MW01125084

The Official Librarian

Bessy's Back!

Bro. Greg,
Thanks for all you
do for our association!
In His Love,
Bro. Nathan ☺

by Nathan Miller

authorHOUSE®

AuthorHouse™
1663 Liberty Drive
Bloomington, IN 47403
www.authorhouse.com
Phone: 1-800-839-8640

First published by AuthorHouse 10/8/2009

ISBN: 978-1-4490-2391-1 (sc)

Printed in the United States of America
Bloomington, Indiana

This book is printed on acid-free paper.

Dedicated to:

Juanita Herrington- my librarian at
Harrison County High School...

Thanks to my Favorite Author, who has written the
Masterpiece of all literature. His Book really talks!
I appreciate the gifts of creativity and imagination
He blesses me with. I don't have a life verse because
they're all good, but check out Romans 10:9-10 in
a Bible to see some of His life-changing writing.

Chapter 1

RING!...RING!...RING!

"Hello," Bessy Beebody said as she laid her tattered book of Sherlock Holmes mysteries on the coffee table after having answered the phone. She looked at her Mickey Mouse watch to check the time and walked towards a blue chair.

"Whoops!... Oh I'm fine, Mom. I just tripped on this old rug. I'm really glad you called. This is the big day you know. I hope I don't mess up... I know all those other times were accidents, but it seems like those kind of crazy things happen wherever I go... O.K., Mom. I won't worry... Yes, I promise. By the way, I've got some neat news for you! Mr. Jacobs, the principal, called me last night and said that the very first copy of Mark Twain's *The Adventures of Huckleberry Finn* is going to be coming to the library today. The book's going to high schools all over America on a tour to promote reading, and we get it first! I want to try to get to school early since they're not sure what time it's going to arrive... Of course it's worth a lot of money... Yeah, I suppose someone could get the idea to steal it, but who would do something like that in Balloonsboro?

I'd better get going. I can't be late the first day... O.K. Bye, Mom." Bessy carefully hung her phone up.

Responsibility was on Bessy's shoulders. She had finally finished her schooling at the University of Bookingham and was now prepared to begin working at the Balloonsboro High School Library as a 100% pure and genuine Official Librarian. This was the day that Bessy Beebody was to begin her new career, and to be honest, she was quite nervous about the whole ordeal she would soon be facing. Regardless of her feelings, however, she was determined to be the best Official Librarian there had ever been.

To make a good impression, Bessy decided to wear something special so she would stand out from the rest of the crowd. She was rather displeased about the selection in her bedroom closet. One thing was too flashy; one was too ordinary; one was too gaudy; and another, too old fashioned. Bessy's alarm clock ticked on as she disapprovingly flipped through garments she had owned since she was a teenager. Unfortunately, nothing seemed to fit the crucial role she was going to play. Bessy eventually ended her search and decided to make a pit stop at the dress shop in town on her way to work. She remembered that there was a gorgeous blouse and skirt on sale for half price, which would be just right for an Official Librarian. Since Bessy was only going to the dress store that her friend owned, she decided to wear the old clothes she had on. After all, there was no sense in putting something uncomfortable on before she had to.

After Bessy had gobbled down a cinnamon twist pastry, she swiftly went back to her bedroom to do some lady-stuff so she could become a flawless creature and hopefully impress her co-workers. When the make-up period was over, the hair grooming period began. The mirror on the wall showed Bessy as the epitome of a pauper, clothes-wise that is. The new outfit she planned on buying would change this, however. As Bessy arranged her golden brown hair, she daydreamed about the first time she attended Balloonsboro High as a freshman. Eventually, the hair fiddling was finished and Bessy sat down to rest.

"Ohhhhh my poor belly!" Bessy groaned.

Bessy, who was a very jittery person, had worried herself until she got an upset stomach. Her tummy roared and growled like a caged lion. The cinnamon twist seemed to be pushing against her insides. It was trying to get out! First it moved in one direction and then the other. The rude pastry made a frantic swishing back and forth. It continuously irritated Bessy Beebody's belly.

"Ohhh, ohhhhh, help, help!" Bessy cried as she unsuccessfully tried to stop the pain by placing her hands over the pastry-infected area. The cinnamon twist was so merciless that Bessy had to go and lie down on her bed. It looked like it was going to be one of those days that Bessy had experienced quite often. You know, the ones that we all have every so often where everything that could go wrong does go wrong.

"I don't have time for a bellyache today," Bessy said. As she stared up at the ceiling and rubbed her tummy, a big, fat, black spider with long, skinny legs crawled towards the light fixture. Bessy liked spiders just about as much as Little Miss Muffet did. Not wasting any time, Bessy picked her sore belly up and trudged into the utility room where she quickly found a can of Bug Terminator insect killer. Now she was ready for action.

After Bessy made it back to her bedroom, she threatened the spider. "All right, you ugly spider! Now you're gonna get it!" Bessy said as she raised her can of bug killer in the air and pushed the button. Bug Terminator sprayed all over poor Bessy. She had aimed the nozzle in the wrong direction. As Bessy coughed and gasped for air, the spider escaped by climbing into a little hole near the light fixture which led into the attic. Bessy now smelled like bug killer. It really didn't matter much about her clothes since she was planning on changing them before she got to work anyway, but her best and only pair of shoes were now quite sticky due to all of the Bug Terminator that had been squirted on just about everything in the bedroom except the spider.

Bessy knew there wasn't enough time to wash her shoes, and she obviously couldn't wear them in the condition they were in, for they had acquired a very nasty odor and an appearance to match. Unfortunately, poor Bessy had cleaned up her house recently and donated all of her spare shoes to the Salvation Army in order to receive a free Cat In The Hat Christmas Countdown Calendar. There were no other choices. Bessy would have to buy another pair of shoes at the dress shop. Fortunately for her, the dress shop had a bountiful supply of footwear. After Bessy got her thoughts together and left her house, she hopped into her red station wagon barefoot and sloppy-looking and sped away towards her friend's dress shop like a crazy race car driver.

Chapter 2

In about ten minutes Bessy arrived downtown and located a parking space in front of the Balloonsboro Post Office. As the soon-to-be Official Librarian got out of her car and shut the door, being cautious to obey the tiny signs that told people not to walk on the grass, she noticed a larger sign. Uncle Sam, who was impolitely pointing his wrinkled finger, supposedly wanted Bessy to join the Air Force. Bessy just ignored him. She wasn't about to work for anyone with such bad manners. Bessy often wondered how the signs were ever placed where they were if nobody was allowed to walk on the grass. The bell of the courthouse clock struck the hour and reminded Bessy that today there were more important matters to be concerned with, like getting a new dress and some clean shoes before school started and Mark Twain's book arrived.

As Bessy walked towards Patricia's Pantyland Plus, the town's only clothing store for women, a gruff voice startled her. "Hello, Bessy."

Bessy turned around to see who was addressing her. "Well, hi, Mr. Blab," Bessy said.

"How are you today, Bessy? Isn't this a lovely day? You know this is the ideal time of the year for a picnic?

I hate it when it's hot. Don't you? I can't stand hot weather. It just makes me sweat something dreadful. Cold weather is just as bad, though. I haven't seen you for so long. Where in the world have you been, Bessy?"

"Well, Mr. ..." Bessy unsuccessfully attempted to say something.

"Oh never mind, Bessy, it's not important. Did you watch all of those riots on T.V. last night? I never saw anything like it in my life. What's the world coming to anyway? Everything is in such a terrible mess. Our street is full of potholes. It looks like somebody has been throwing grenades. I called that no good for nothing city commissioner and gave him a piece of my mind yesterday."

"That shouldn't have taken very long," Bessy murmured under her breath as she looked at her watch.

"I tell you one thing, Bessy. I'll never vote for him again. He's not good for anything at all. Did I tell you about our daughter Jane? She came over last night with some great news about some sort of school job that was available. She's so sweet, isn't she, Bessy? I'd do anything for her. She's my baby."

Bessy bit her tongue as she listened to Mr. Blab blab on. Jane and Bessy had gone to school together. Bessy had a different opinion of Jane. Bessy thought that she was a mean, lying, two-faced, sneaky, selfish, self-centered, snob who talked as much as her dad.

Mr. Blab continued talking. "We had a yard sale last weekend, Bessy. You should have come. I never saw such a crowd in my whole life. I bet at least three hundred people were there. I always enjoy yard sales. They're so much fun!"

Whoopdy doo! Bessy thought as she tapped her watch with her fingernail, hoping Mr. Blab would get the message.

"My uncle called this morning," Mr. Blab said. "He said he's going on a little vacation with his family to Buffaloes's Bunions for a couple of days. You should meet him some time. He's thinking about buying a new house."

Bessy was getting quite frustrated with Mr. Blab. After she had listened to all she could stand, she blurted out, "Good day, sir!" and went on her way. Whether Mr. Blab heard her or not, she didn't know and really didn't care. As Bessy paraded down the street, Mr. Blab continued talking as if she were still there.

The already dark sky gradually became even more rain-threatening in appearance. Noticing this, Bessy picked up her pace considerably. She had already had one shower today, and as far as she was concerned, one a day was enough. As Bessy approached Patricia's, she felt overcome with joy. When she got to the front door, she placed her hand on the handle and kept moving forward.

SPLAT!

Bessy hit her face against the window. Her nose began bleeding. "Shoot fire! What's wrong with this blasted door?" Bessy said.

Bessy tried frantically to unjam the door. She pushed, shoved, and pulled until her hands became sore. Bessy yanked a tissue from her pocket and tenderly wiped her injured nose. It felt like it was broken. Bessy couldn't understand what was wrong with the door. It had never given her any trouble before. Usually it was so simple to open. Bessy peeked inside the store and discovered that the lights were all off.

"Maybe Pat's not here yet," Bessy said as she wiped her nose again and fearfully glanced down at her watch. Mickey Mouse's arms were moving faster than Bessy wanted them to move.

When Bessy looked back up, she noticed something horrifying hanging in the side window. It was a cardboard sign that read: CLOSED TWO WEEKS FOR VACATION. "Well isn't this a sight for sore eyes! And sore noses too!" Bessy whined, "What am I going to do now?"

There were no other dress shops in town. Even though Bessy resembled a tramp, she couldn't go back to her house without risking being late for work and possibly missing the arrival of Mark Twain's famous book. Besides, Bessy had a reputation for always being on time. She had even been born at the exact time the doctor had predicted. Bessy had never been late in her life, and today wasn't going to be the first time. She would have to go to work dressed as she was. Bessy unenthusiastically jogged back to her station wagon and began to open the door.

CLICK!

"Oh no!" Bessy cried. "It's locked!" As she peered through the window on the driver's side of her station wagon, she saw her keys hanging from the ignition like trapezists.

Chapter 3

The clouds that were previously grayish rapidly became a dark blue and hovered over the town as the hands on the courthouse clock continued to move.

KABOOM! All of a sudden a loud clap of thunder sounded and the clouds over Balloonsboro began dropping rain. There Bessy sat on the street corner, depressed as an alligator in Antarctica. Raindrops kept falling on Bessy's head as she humiliatingly watched two firemen who were trying to unlock her car door. Bessy had never had to call the fire department in her life... until now, that is.

While Bessy sat in the rain, watching the firemen wrestle with her lock and wondering if she would be late for work, a young dalmatian trotted up from behind her and graciously presented her with a couple of wet ones across her mouth and nose.

"Ahhh, ohh yuck! That's gross, you dumb dog!" Bessy shouted as she swatted her hand at the overly friendly animal and wiped the dog spit from her lips. "Skat, dog! Get away from me!" The dog ignored Bessy and lay down right beside her. "You dumb old dog!" Bessy said.

Bessy glanced at her watch as the dog rubbed its rear end up against her side and made playful gestures with its eyes. Meanwhile, the firemen were still working with her lock. Bessy noticed two children playing across the street from her. They looked so cute and innocent. The rain kept falling.

POP!

Bessy jumped. One of the cute, innocent kids had just thrown a rock and hit one of the firemen in the head. The fireman ignored the brat since his fire helmet had protected him from injury. Bessy sighed impatiently as she looked to her right side. The dalmatian that had kissed her on the lips a few moments earlier was now biting at fleas. In order to escape from her four-legged friend's company, Bessy decided to take a short stroll down the street. When she returned, her car door was unlocked.

The firemen were true lifesavers. Not only did they unlock Bessy's car door, but they also gave her a pair of old fire boots to wear when they noticed she was barefoot. After Bessy had kindly thanked the nice men several times, she hopped back into her station wagon and proceeded toward the high school and her new job. It only took her about five minutes to get where she was going since Balloonsboro wasn't a very large town.

When Bessy had parked, she turned her car off and carefully took her keys out of the ignition to put them in her purse. But where was her purse? She distinctly remembered taking it with her when she left the house. It wasn't anywhere to be seen now, though.

"This is ridiculous," Bessy said. "I know I had my purse earlier. Oh, I remember. I threw it in the backseat."

Bessy leaned back to get her purse. All of a sudden she jumped up out of the car seat and hit her head on the ceiling. Something had bitten her on the finger. When Bessy turned around to see what had attacked her pinky, she almost fainted. There in the backseat lay the impolite dalmatian who had gotten fresh with her earlier. As if that wasn't bad enough, the dog was chewing on Bessy's good pocketbook.

"Look what you've done, you monster! I don't have time for this!" Bessy screamed. "How did you get in here, you beast? How dare you chew on my good purse!"

The dog made no reply. Bessy swiftly drew her ice scraper from the glove compartment, better than King Arthur himself could have drawn his sword, and ferociously kicked open the car door with her fireboots. She immediately and desperately began to scrape and pull on the dog as if he were a giant snowflake stuck on her windshield. The dalmatian barked at her in a vicious tone and slapped her sore nose with his smelly tail. Bessy, now furious, grabbed the dog and got him in a head-lock. The dog escaped by using a secret maneuver. He gave Bessy another dog sugar, right on the lips again. After a couple of minutes had gone by, which seemed like hours to Bessy, she had somehow managed to drag the dirty creature from her vehicle. She then unsuccessfully kicked at the dog's hind end with one of her fireboots, but missed and fell down on her bottom. The dog just grinned and trotted away.

"No good for nothing mutt!" Bessy muttered as she looked at her watch. "If he was mine, I'd send him to the pound! That dirty, stinking dog!"

Bessy began to salvage the remains of what used to be her good purse. The purse was no longer the same, however, for the dog had transformed it into something very unique. It was now full of teethmarks and one strap was torn off. The purse looked like it had been dropped into an aquarium full of piranhas. Most of Bessy's belongings were now ruined. Her plastic hair spray bottle now had a big hole and was leaking all over the floor mat. The dog had bent Bessy's sunglasses, tore up her rain bonnet, and slobbered on her billfold.

Portions of her make-up had been eaten, and her hand lotion had become paw lotion. Bessy threw the remains into the unusual pocket book and got out of her car, making sure she had her keys. Then she slammed the car door, walked over to the building, and entered the school after she amazingly opened the door with ease.

The Balloonsboro High School was old and dreary looking on the inside. It was neither too big nor too small. It was middle-sized. Bessy headed straight to the office to check in as the Official Librarian. It had finally quit raining outside. Bessy gathered her thoughts. Maybe today would turn out all right after all. What else could possibly go wrong? Before Bessy was able to convince herself that the rest of the day might be better, she passed two students who pointed and laughed after they looked at her.

Chapter 4

B essy quietly entered the office, where she found a fairly young looking lady with glasses sitting behind a metal desk.

"Just a moment please. I'll be right with you," the secretary said in a soft voice.

To pass time, Bessy studied the place. The walls were a light shade of brown. A picture of George Washington hung above a copying machine, and to the right of the cherry tree-chopping President was a nail that firmly held a thick wooden paddle, probably used by the principal for practical purposes. Bessy noticed there were letters engraved on the paddle. She laughed when she read them to herself. "Beware! The Board of Education Will Get You In The End." This was a typical school office. The wall appeared to be textured, but when Bessy touched it she discovered that it was actually a white wall hidden by brown dust.

"All right now, can I help you?" the secretary asked.

"Why, yes, I'm the new Official Librarian," Bessy said.

"Really? You're not joking are you, dear?" the secretary asked as she closely examined Bessy with her eyes.

"Of course not!" Bessy said.

"Well then, just go in that door over there, and Mr. Jacobs, the principal, will talk with you. You're Bessy Beebody. Right?"

"That's right."

"I'm Grace Dover. I used to work with your aunt."

"I remember hearing her talk about you. She really misses you."

"I know. I miss her as well, but this job is a lot better. I don't want to make you late. Maybe I'll stop by the library around lunch and we can chat."

"Sounds good to me."

"Well, Mr. Jacobs is in there waiting for you. I'll see you on the way out."

"O.K.," Bessy said as she nervously stepped into the principal's office. She hoped that the childhood rhyme about the principal being one's pal was true for Official Librarians. Bessy's stomach began growling as she found herself in front of a jolly looking fellow with a mustache. He was sitting in a chair behind an oak desk smoking a pipe. To some degree, the smoke circled his head like a wreath. This was how Bessy had always pictured Santa Claus as a young man. The principal spoke to her. "Come in, come in. Have a seat. Are you Bessy Beebody?"

"Yes sir, Mr. Jacobs. I'm Bussy... I mean Bessy Beebody."

"Just call me Joe. Let's get straight to business. First of all, we have a library and you are an Official Librarian. You come very highly recommended." Mr. Jacobs stared at Bessy a minute and twisted his mustache. "I have checked your records, and you seem to have no apparent flaws." Mr. Jacobs looked at Bessy again with a devilish grin.

"Is something wrong with me, Mr. Jacobs?" Bessy asked.

"Joe remember. Joe."

"I mean, Joe, is there something wrong with me?"

"No, Bessy. It's just, uh... are you a volunteer fireman by any chance?"

"Why no. Of course not."

"Oh. I just thought that... Oh well, these new fads just keep getting weirder and weirder."

Then it hit her. Bessy had completely forgotten about her physical appearance. There she was, dressed like a tramp. Mr. Jacobs, Grace Dover, and the kids in the hall all had good reason to look and laugh at Bessy Beebody. Bessy's hair was wet and tangled. She dripped rain on the floor when she made the slightest movement. Her eyes were very dark and bloodshot, much like those of a drug abuser's. Bessy's body smelled like some odd combination of bug spray, mildew, sweat, and dirty dog. Her nose now had a reddish coloration, and her hands were in desperate need of a skin doctor due to all the fighting she had done with the dress shop door. Just by glancing at her, one would have thought her boss was the director of a horror movie.

Her clothes didn't do much for her looks either. Bessy was wearing an old blue sweatshirt with grease spots all over it that her uncle had given her for Christmas one year. The shirt was covered with slogans. On the front it read, "Nuke The Russians Before They Rush The Nukins" and on the back, "Save The Whales, Please Contribute To Weight Watchers Generously." Bessy's legs were covered by a pair of extremely loose blue jeans that had holes in both knees. The back of the jeans were very dirty from where she had sat on the street corner earlier that day. On her arm hung what had been her good purse. To make matters worse, she had those dreadful looking fireboots on her Official Librarian tootsies. That was probably why Mr. Jacobs inquired if Bessy was a fire fighter. To sum things up, Bessy looked like she had just taken an airplane ride through a hurricane, with the windows down.

Mr. Jacobs continued talking. "Well, Bessy, if you don't have any questions... I guess you can get to work. Here's your Official Library Key. I'll say one thing. You sure are a change from our last librarian. I'll try to get in touch with you later to discuss the plans for when Mark Twain's book arrives. I don't know what time it will get here yet. They're supposed to call me, so I'll let you know when they let me know. I'm sure you must be delighted to have such a distinguished literary work coming here."

"I certainly am, Joe. It really is great for both the kids and the teachers."

"If you need anything at all, Bessy, be sure to let me know."

"I sure will."

"Good luck, Bessy."

Bessy smiled. "Thank you. I'll see you later."

Bessy took a deep breath and headed towards the library after she received directions and a few pointers from Grace Dover. Although Bessy's clothes weren't very becoming, she was now the Official Librarian of the Balloonsboro High School, and she now had the Official Library Key to prove it.

Chapter 5

B essy stumbled into the library. Just like the office, it too was very dusty. Paper wads and other student litter covered the floor like an ocean. Bessy had never been in such a filthy place in her life. The library resembled a warzone. Books were cluttered in anti-alphabetical order on every shelf, like wind blown-leaves. On one wall by the fiction section, someone had spray painted graffiti. It read: "Kill The Librarian," and was accompanied with a frightful picture of a woman with a noose around her neck. Bessy was so upset that she wanted to grow horns and blow smoke. Suddenly, the title of Official Librarian seemed to lose all the glamour it had previously possessed.

"Things could be worse I suppose," Bessy said. "I'd better try to clean this mess up a bit before the book gets here," Bessy whined as she shrugged her shoulders and glanced at her watch.

After she grabbed some cleaning materials from the closet, Bessy went to work. She began by dusting. First she took care of her Official Desk, and then she started on the bookshelves and books. The dust was very thick in some places. Over where the Bibles were kept, the dust had formed layers. Behind the holy books, Bessy discovered two dead cockroaches. It was obvious that the discovery was very ancient, for both roaches had wrinkles and gray hair to match. As Bessy wiped and whined, unhappy tribes of spiders were forced to move elsewhere. What had been their home for so long was now becoming Bessy's clean bookshelf.

Bessy's hand continued to move in a circular motion until the majority of the dust was removed from the shelf she was concentrating on. As she was putting a misplaced book where it belonged, Bessy noticed an interesting cook book. Having a taste for good food, she opened it. A terrible thing was discovered on page 22, directly between Reida's Ravishing Raw Ravioli Rolls and Rhonda's Rhino Relish. Some doofus had spat his tobacco remains in the poor, defenseless book. Bessy mumbled unkind words to the person who did the dastardly deed and furiously wiped the book off as well as she could. When finished, she walked over to the next shelf. As she dusted, she sang for her own entertainment. At first her music made little sense, but after she got warmed up, it made even less sense.

"La Da Doo Da Da Dy Doo Da Doody Daddy Doo Doo, I ain't nothin but a hound dog!" Bessy sang. She imagined herself in front of a large audience. All eyes were on her. Unfortunately for the audience, Bessy Beebody couldn't carry a tune in a bucket to save her life. The best solo she would ever sing would be so low that nobody could hear it. To make matters worse, Bessy had a terrible memory when it came to song lyrics. Thus, she combined just about every song she'd ever heard in her life into one giant tear-jerking masterpiece of comedy. "This little light of mine, I'm gonna let it shine, Summertime summertime sum sum summertime, Happy birthday to you, happy birthday to you, you look like a monkey and smell like one too."

Suddenly Bessy's unforgettable concert was interrupted. Someone had entered the library. Bessy slowly turned around to look at her first customer. "Ahhhh, Ahhhhh! Help! Stay away!" Bessy screamed as she dashed over to the corner and jumped on top of the old card catalog like a wild kangaroo. A big hairy gorilla with shiny white teeth was standing in the doorway.

"Get away!" Bessy shouted. "Ahhhhhh! Help me somebody!"

The overgrown monkey ignored Bessy's request and tromped closer and closer toward her.

Bessy felt faint. Her knees began to shake, and a cold chill ran down her spine. "Stay away I said! Back! Get back! Leave me alone and I'll give you all the bananas you want! Please stay back!"

"What's wrong, Bessy?" the gorilla asked.

"Oh no. Don't tell me you talk. I suppose you want to check out a book, Mr. Gorilla? How in the world do you know my name?"

"I'm Harold Harpelander, the vice-principal," the Gorilla explained.

"I've heard of equal rights, but this is ridiculous."

"I'm not really a gorilla, Bessy. This is just a costume for my wife's Wildlife Day costume party. I went in the restroom to try it on, and I got the zipper stuck. I wonder if I could borrow your scissors to degorillaize myself?"

"Sure. I believe there's a pair of scissors over there on my desk."

The gorilla stomped over to the desk and fixed his zipper. A partially bald-headed vice-principal popped out of the gorilla suit and laid the scissors back on the desk while the Official Librarian cautiously watched from the top of the card catalog. Bessy noticed that the man's gray hair made a horseshoe design on his head.

"Well, I guess my wife can work with this so it won't keep getting stuck," the vice-principal said. "Thanks for the use of your scissors."

"You're welcome."

"Did you like my costume, Bessy?"

"Oh, it was really shocking."

"Well, thank you. I guess I'd better be leaving. Before I go, you probably should get off the card catalog, Bessy. Didn't your parents ever tell you not to stand on the furniture? You're setting a bad example for the students. I don't think Mr. Jacobs would be very thrilled if he saw you up there either. I'll see you later."

Bessy rapidly climbed down from Mount Card Catalog with a bright red face. She was embarrassed and angry at the same time. After she recovered from her frightening encounter with King Kong, she noticed the clock on the wall and quickly went back to work. Bessy aimed to have a tidy library before The Adventures of Huckleberry Finn arrived. When she finished cleaning the dictionaries, she unsuccessfully attempted to move on to the encyclopedias. Bessy felt something was holding her foot down to the floor. She tried to pull her foot loose several times, but it wouldn't budge. Finally she made one desperate tug, using all of her lingering cinnamon twist pastry energy.

SMACK!

Bessy yanked the fireboot she was wearing up from the floor, kicking herself in the face and falling flat down on her bottom for the second time that day. Luckily she didn't knock herself out or cause her already-injured nose to start bleeding again. Bessy glanced at the sole of her fireboot to see what had held her foot down so tightly. The villain turned out to be a large hunk of purple bubble gum. It dangled from Bessy's heel like a piece of spaghetti. After Bessy cleaned her boot off, she began cleaning the encyclopedias. They were in terrible shape for the most part.

When Bessy opened one of the reference books, a piece of folded notebook paper fell onto the floor. A naughty drawing was sketched on the outside of the paper. Bessy picked it up and peeked inside. She read it to herself.

"Dear Deloris,

I can't do without you. I haven't seen you since last night, honey. Please be my sugar pig, honey. I love you, sugar. I really do. Won't you be mine, baby?"

The letter went on, but Bessy couldn't. She wadded it up and pitched it in the trash can. "Good grief!" Bessy said. "What have I gotten myself into? I feel more like the Official Zookeeper than the Official Librarian."

Before Bessy had time to pick up another book, Grace Dover's voice came from the speaker on the library wall. "Bessy, could you please come to the office for a minute. Mr. Jacobs needs to see you."

"Sure. I'll be right there," Bessy said.

Chapter 6

Bessy was as happy as a bee in a honey factory on her way back from the office. Mr. Jacobs had given her great news. The Adventures of Huckleberry Finn would be arriving around 1:00 p.m. Before she left school, Bessy would have the pleasure of personally looking at the very first copy of one of Mark Twain's most well-known books. As if that wasn't enough good news by itself, Mr. Jacobs also surprised Bessy by informing her that she would be getting some much needed help. The school had hired a temporary worker to help Bessy guard the famous book that would soon be in her library. To top that off, Bessy also would be getting an Official Librarian's Student Aide. Bessy was so happy when Mr. Jacobs told her all the good news that she forgot to ask him who the new workers were. It didn't matter, however, for things seemed to be going great. Bessy did know that she wouldn't get to meet the temporary worker until the book arrived. That person had been sent by the school superintendent to meet the people who were going to deliver the famous book to Balloonsboro High. Bessy's new student aide was supposed to be in the library by the time she got back from the office, though. She could hardly wait to meet him or her. How fun it would be to have a nice young man or woman to help with the library chores.

Bessy gracefully popped into the library with scanning eyes. Her expectations for her new student aide were so high that she wasn't even thinking straight. There had been so much cleaning to do that she had just about worn herself out. Now things might be a little easier, if not a lot. Bessy's scanning continued. Her head revolved like a broken roulette wheel, back and forth to no avail. Where was her new aide anyway? Mr. Jacobs said that he or she should be in the library. Bessy Beebody, as usual, was baffled. She attempted the frantic search once more. Bessy concluded that her aide hadn't arrived yet and began to move towards her Official Desk.

BUMP! Bessy had hit something, just like the Titanic, only on a smaller scale. She abruptly stopped her motor and looked down to see what she had walked into. A baseball cap appeared to be floating over the floor. Bessy blinked her eyes and looked again. The cap raised up and revealed a small boy's face which held two blue eyes, a small mouth, and a runny nose with freckles.

The small mouth opened. "Hi."

Bessy retreated a bit and responded. "Hi."

The two looked at each other for a couple of seconds. Bessy felt like Goliath talking to David. The boy was extremely tiny. At most he was four feet tall.

"I'm the librarian. Who are you?" Bessy asked the little boy.

"I'm the new student aide," he answered.

Bessy was somewhat flabbergasted. Her high hopes had been shot down by life's anti-aircraft guns.

"What grade are you in?" Bessy asked.

"I should be in the first grade, but I passed some tests and got moved up."

"Oh, I see. Well what's your name? Mine is Bessy Beebody."

The little boy looked up at Bessy and quietly said, "Idunno."

"What do you mean you don't know, honey? You can tell me."

"Idunno."

"I want to be your friend, and a friend has to know another friend's name. Right?"

"I suppose so," the boy agreed.

"Well then, tell me your name."

"Idunno," the boy said.

"O.K. then," Bessy said, "if you won't tell me your first name, then you surely would tell me your last name. What's your last name?"

"Nothin."

"What do you mean nothin? Don't you have a last name, honey?"

"Yes, mam."

"Well then, what's your last name?"

"Nothin."

Bessy calmly grew angry. She decided to try to trick the boy.

"When your mom calls you for supper, what does she yell?" Bessy asked.

"Idunno!"

"You mean to say that you don't even know what your mom yells when she calls you for supper?"

"No. I know what she yells."

"What does she yell?"

"Idunno!"

"O.K. then. Tell me your whole name, first and last together."

"Idunno Nothin."

"Surely you know your name if you skipped from kindergarten to high school. Are you trying to drive me crazy or something?"

"Nope."

"Well then, for the final time, tell me your whole name."

"My name is Idunno Nothin. Look here." The boy pulled a card out of his hip pocket that had a picture on it and handed it to Bessy.

"What's this?" Bessy asked.

"It's my Balloonsboro Brilliant Brat's Club membership card."

Bessy read the card. "Oh, my goodness! So your name is Idunno Nothin. I'm sorry," Bessy said.

"I thought you were Bessy. Just joking," the youngster said with a grin.

"I guess I deserve it. Sorry I took so long to understand you," Bessy said.

"That's all right. It happens all the time."

"I'm just a little curious, Idunno. If I'm not being too nosy, could you tell me your middle name?"

"Of course. My middle name is Muchyoudoabout."

"So your full name is Idunno Muchyoudoabout Nothin?"

"Well, actually it's Idunno Muchyoudoabout Nothin the third."

"Well, Idunno," Bessy said, "you can just call me Bessy."

"O.K."

"Come over here to my desk and I'll show you how you can help."

Idunno politely followed Bessy's request and the Official Librarian's Student Aide Training Program began.

Chapter 7

At about 9:30 a.m. an English class began pouring into the library. They were accompanied by a slim, blond haired woman who appeared to be in her early thirties. She was carrying a baseball bat in her right hand. After making a timid entrance, the class quietly sat down at the library tables like trained dogs. Bessy listened as the teacher gave her students their orders. "All right, children. You know what to do. Remember your book must be written by a contemporary author. I don't want to hear any whispering whatsoever. If anybody causes any trouble, you know what I'm going to do?"

"Yes, mam," the group answered together.

"Are there any questions?" the teacher asked.

"No, mam," the class replied.

"Then get to work, you scoundrels!" she yelled. Immediately the students jumped up from their seats and ran to the bookshelves.

As the students shuffled around the room, the teacher put her baseball bat under a chair and marched over towards Bessy. Bessy unenthusiastically waited for her arrival. If she could have vanished, she would have. Bessy tried to act busy by looking at her desk calendar.

"Are you the new librarian?" the teacher asked. Bessy was overcome by a horrible stench. Obviously the woman talking to Bessy had never heard of mouthwash.

"Yes. I am," Bessy said, breathing through her mouth to avoid inhaling the smelly fumes from the mean teacher's mouth.

"Well, I'm Wartella Snollygoster, the head of the English department. What's your name?" The odor increased.

"My name is Bessy Beebody."

"That sure is a peculiar name. I think I've heard it somewhere before. Oh, I remember. My neighbors used to have a dog named Bessy."

"That's nice," Bessy said as she tried to ignore the woman and hold her breath at the same time.

"Hope you have more sense than that dog did. She was the biggest fool I've ever seen in my life," the teacher said.

Bessy began to get put out with the rude woman. "Is there something you wanted?" Bessy asked as she looked down at Mickey Mouse's arms and daydreamed about what it would be like when Twain's book arrived.

"Yes, there is," Wartella said. "Do you have any of the new magazines in yet?"

"Idunno," Bessy said. Idunno, the new student aide, came running over to Bessy.

"Did you want me?" Idunno asked Bessy.

"No, Idunno. I was talking to Ms. Snollygoster," Bessy said.

"Oh. Sorry," he said.

"That's all right," Bessy said as her little helper went back to what he was doing. "I don't know if the new magazines are in yet or not," Bessy said to Wartella. "I just got here today, and I haven't had a chance to get the mail from the office yet."

"That figures," Wartella said.

"What do you mean?" Bessy asked.

"It figures that someone new, like you, wouldn't have enough sense to go and pick up the mail."

"How dare you talk to me like that," Bessy said.

Mr. Jacobs, the principal, entered the library while the kids quietly watched.

"Oooo!" Wartella said. "Aren't we touchy today?"

"No, I'm not touchy. Any normal human being wouldn't be as impolite as you've been Snollygoster. If you want to talk about peculiar names, why don't you start with your own?"

"You think you're something special, don't you, Bessy Beebody? Nobody can smartmouth Wartella Snollygoster and get away with it. You just wait and see. I'll make you wish you'd never come to Balloonsboro High."

"Make my day, Snolly!"

"I sure will, darling!"

"Before you make anyone's day, you'd better buy some mouthwash and shave your mustache," Bessy said.

"That does it!" Wartella Snollygoster shouted.

POW!

Wartella had hit poor Bessy in the jaw with her fist. In return, Bessy shouted, "Now is the winter of your discontent, you old dirty vulture!" as she quickly grabbed the anthology of William Shakespeare from her desk and thrusted it directly at Wartella's face. The heavy book hit Wartella right between the eyes and knocked her out. She fell on the carpet like a dead opossum. The class cheered for Bessy as she raised her arms in victory and looked down at her opponent.

"Fair is foul, and so is your breath," Bessy said. The students laughed and clapped their hands.

While Bessy and the students were celebrating, Mr. Jacobs came up to Bessy and tapped her on the shoulder. "All right, young lady. As soon as Ms. Snollygoster gets

up, I'm taking you both to the office for a little talk."
Suddenly Bessy's victory balloon had been deflated.

Chapter 8

Bessy embarrassingly sat in the school office, attempting to figure out how she got in such a big mess in such a short time. You know how it is when you do something dumb without thinking about it and then you think about how dumb you were to have done it without thinking about it? Directly across from Bessy sat Wartella Snollygoster. Every few minutes Wartella would stare at Bessy with an evil eye and make a snarling gesture with her mouth. Bessy had never been sent to the principal's office in her life. She was wondering if she could be whipped or given detention. How would she explain it to her mom? Bessy wished that Grace Dover was there to comfort her, but she had gone to deliver some papers to one of the elementary schools.

The clock on the wall made a loud ticking noise. Bessy hoped that Mr. Jacobs would hurry up and sentence her before <u>The Adventures of Huckleberry Finn</u> arrived. As she looked up, her eyes met Wartella's. Wartella stuck her tongue out at Bessy. Bessy just ignored the gesture and hoped even harder that the principal would hurry up. Then the office door opened. To Bessy's relief, it was Mr. Jacobs.

"All right, ladies, I apologize for keeping you waiting, but I had somebody on the phone in the other room. You two know that I'm disappointed in you. As faculty we're supposed to set a good example for the students. You two sure weren't doing that. I'm not going to lecture to you all day. The kids keep me busy enough. I just want you to know that I'm not going to have my staff fighting with each other. We have to work together. I'm not going to say anymore on the subject. Now I want you two to shake hands and make up."

Bessy slowly rose from her seat and met Wartella. Bessy held her hand out as Wartella snarled and placed her claw in it, and the two grudgingly made a small shaking motion. Then it was over. There was no paddling and no detention. All Bessy had to do was shake her enemy's hand. After she thought about it for a minute, she wished that she could have exchanged the shake for a whipping or detention. It was too late, though. The phony truce had already been made. All Bessy had to do now was get some soap and water to rinse the scum off her hand and she would be happy once again.

"Well, that's nice," Mr. Jacobs said with a grin. "Now you can go."

Wartella flew out the door like a mad bat, and Bessy began to leave too.

"Wait a minute, Bessy," Mr. Jacobs said. "I need you to stay."

"Oh you do?" Bessy said, wondering if maybe she was still going to get a spanking.

"Yes, I do. Don't worry about this thing with Wartella too much. She can't get along with anybody. To be honest, I'm glad you hit her with the book. She deserved it. She's been picking on just about everybody in the school for years. You're the first one who had enough courage to stand up to her. Hopefully you taught her a lesson. Anyway, that's not what I want to talk to you about. The reason I came to the library in the first place was to give you these papers about Mark Twain's book." He handed her the papers.

Bessy happily looked at them. "This is very interesting," Bessy said. "They tell all about the book, don't they?"

"They sure do. And I also wanted you to know that you'll have your own key to get the book out of its security case in an emergency."

"You better not give me a key. Can't you keep it?" Bessy asked.

"I insist that you have one, Bessy. I trust you. I'm going to have one too. Let's just not use them unless it really is an emergency. I certainly don't want that book to get lost."

"Don't worry. I'll guard it with my life."

"I know you will. If you need any help or have any problems in the future, don't hesitate to come and talk to me."

"Oh, I won't. Before I leave I want to thank you for being so kind about my problem with Ms. Snollygoster."

"That's all right, Bessy. Believe me, I understand. Wartella Snollygoster has hit me before, but I could never hit a lady, even though she doesn't act like one."

"I just want you to know, I really do appreciate your kindness, sir."

"Joe, remember!"

"I'm sorry. I mean, thank you, Joe, for being so understanding."

"You're welcome, Bessy."

Then Bessy Beebody, the Official Librarian, picked her pride back up and headed for the library.

Chapter 9

It was about eleven thirty according to the wall clock in the library. Bessy had to wait only about another hour and a half before Twain's book would arrive. So far Bessy's first day had worn her to a frazzle, and it wasn't even halfway over yet. Bessy's stomach was starting to growl. It was as empty as a poor man's savings account. "I guess it's time to eat," Bessy said as she strolled over to her Official Desk and picked up a brown paper sack which contained the lunch she had ordered from the Balloonsboro Deli. After grabbing her grub, she walked over to a table by the magazine rack and perched her Official bottom on a wooden stool. Suddenly, Grace Dover popped into the library. Bessy's stomach continued to rumble as Grace pranced over to the table.

"How are you doing so far, Bessy?" Grace asked.

"Just fine," Bessy said.

"You don't mind if I join you for lunch, do you?"

"Of course not. Don't be silly. Pull up a seat. I was just getting ready to eat."

Grace pulled a chair over to the table as Bessy opened her brown bag in a respectable manner, which was very fitting for an Official Librarian.

41

"What did you bring to eat today, Grace?" Bessy asked.

"I just brought some fruit cocktail. What about you, dear?"

I ordered a bologna sandwich from the deli. It's one of my favorites."

"Yes, it is rather tasty. I have to eat the fruit cocktail, though. I'm on this all fruit diet you see."

"Why in the world are you on a diet, Grace? You're as skinny as a rail all over."

"You can't see alllllll over, Bes. My rear end won't fit into any of my clothes, and my husband told me that I couldn't buy anything new. He says I just keep outgrowing everything."

Bessy remembered hearing her aunt talk about how Grace's husband wouldn't let her have much money. "Well, I suppose you have to do what you have to do," Bessy said as she arranged her sandwich out on the table. It was an ordinary bologna sandwich. Nothing special. Just a piece of meat between two slices of bread and... But, no. Something terrible was wrong with the sandwich. It was too ordinary and too plain. Bessy removed the top slice of bread. It was an unbearable sight. There was no mayonnaise. Bessy laid the bread to the side of the bologna. "Oh no! Can you believe this? I forgot to ask for mayonnaise!" Bessy said.

"Don't worry about it, Bes. You're better off without the stuff. It's loaded with calories I bet," Grace said.

"It tastes so plain without it, though."

"Do you want some fruit cocktail? It's real good for you."

"No thanks. I was sort of in a bologna and mayo mood."

"Yeah, I know what it's like to get your taste buds all set to eat something and then to have a change in the menu," Grace said.

"I guess I'll just have to do without. Do you think it's hot in here?" Bessy asked her friend.

"It sure is," Grace said. "Why don't you open that window behind you? It might just cool this place off a little bit."

"That's a good idea." Bessy walked over to the lockless window and opened it halfway. Surprisingly, it gave her no trouble at all, unlike the dress shop door she had tangled with earlier. Bessy, proud of her accomplishment, strutted back to the table and sat back down with her new friend and her plain sandwich.

"I heard about you thumping old Snollygoster with that book today. The whole school is talking about it," Grace said.

While Grace talked about Bessy and Wartella Snollygoster's fight, Bessy dreamed about punishing herself for ordering an unmayonnaised sandwich. One minute, she pictured herself in a torture chamber. A tiny bald headed man hit her in the face with a stick and repeatedly yelled: "How dare you forget the mayonnaise!"

The next minute, Bessy found herself in a dark, spooky forest. A wizard in a mayonnaise colored robe casually strolled up to Bessy and began a conversation with her. "Good day, madam," he said. "Welcome to Balstar. There are many deadly creatures roaming around here. Be careful or you shall die for sure."

"How can I save myself?" Bessy screamed in horror.

"There is only one thing that will stop the creatures."

"Please tell me, Mr. Wizard. What must I do?"

"All right, my fair maiden. In order to keep the monsters from eating you, you must give them a bologna sandwich with mayonnaise."

"No wizard! Not that! You see, I don't have any mayonnaise. I forgot to order it."

"I'm sorry, my dear. Then you must die. Farewell."

The wizard slowly faded out of sight. Bessy yelled for him to stay. "Don't go! Please stay! Don't leave me here all alone!"

Suddenly, hoards of ugly, winged monsters leaped down out of trees that encircled the Official Librarian. The monsters rudely knocked Bessy down and began nibbling on her arms and legs.

Bessy frantically called for the wizard. "Please don't go! Don't leave me! Please stay!"

I have to, Bes," Grace said. "Mr. Jacobs will get upset if I don't go back on time."

Bessy blinked her eyes and looked at the clock on the wall. "O.K., Grace. I'll see you later."

"Bye, Bes. Oh, I almost forgot. Mr. Jacobs wants you to meet him at the front of the building around one o'clock for the book's arrival."

"I sure will, Grace. I'm really looking forward to seeing what it looks like."

"You and every other faculty member in the school just about."

"Really, Grace?"

"Really. Mr. Jacobs has got everybody excited."

"That's great."

"I'd better go and let you get prepared. Let me know after they get it set up in the security case so I can come and see it. I always did think Twain had a nifty sense of humor. I really did enjoy eating with you, Bes. I sure wish that I ate like you do. If I did, then I surely wouldn't have to worry about my clothes fitting. See ya later."

The wall clock continued to tick. Soon the famous book would be in the library. Would Bessy have enough strength to protect it without eating lunch, though? Bessy looked down at the table as Grace walked out the door. There lay her bologna sandwich with the top off. No mayonnaise was present. Bessy's stomach growled at her. After Grace had left, Bessy began to ponder about her mayonnaiseless predicament. Before she was able to examine her dilemma in great depths, her chain of thought was abruptly broken. A middle-sized robin darted in the open window like a jet. It startled Bessy at first. "Oh my goodness sakes alive!" Bessy said.

The bird hovered throughout the library as if it were a new student taking a tour of the facilities. Eventually, the bird settled down and landed on the Official Librarian's Desk. Bessy immediately ran to the back storage room and returned carrying a cardboard box. Slowly she crept toward the unsuspecting bird. When Bessy was close to the desk, she paused and gave the bird a pep talk. "Nice bird. Good birdy. That's a good birdy." Then without warning, Bessy the mighty hunter sprang forward and slammed the box down on the desk. The bird was more than good and nice. He was very quick and intelligent. Birdy was too fast for Bessy, even if she was an Official Librarian. Before the box ever had time to hit the desk top, the bird had shot off like a bottle rocket, only to begin his frivolous fluttering once more.

Neither Bessy nor the bird was very happy at this time. There Bessy was with a wild bird flying around in her library, with an embarrassing thought flying around in her mind that the priceless book she had been waiting to see so long might arrive at any moment. What was she to do? Things were even worse from the bird's point of view. He had accidently flown into the open window and entered a strange new world which didn't fancy his feathers. To make matters worse, he was now unable to find the exit and a peculiar looking woman who smelled like bug spray was trying to capture him in a cardboard box.

    As the bird flew around, Bessy got a brilliant idea. This was an event which rarely occurred. Bessy quickly ran to the storage room once more and came back out waving a broom. She began swatting at the bird. If it wasn't for the bird, Bessy would have appeared to have been cleaning the ceiling. "Good bird, the window's over here bird," Bessy said. The bird flapped and chirped as Bessy's broom came after him. His chirps were full of bad words. Finally, the bird noticed the window and zipped over the lunch table and back outside where he belonged.

Then Bessy put her bird-busting equipment up and closed the window without a lock, in order to avoid further animal encounters. The library had been relieved of a fugitive. Bessy walked back to the table where she had been daydreaming and sat down once more. She sighed as she glanced where her lunch had been, but it was no longer there. "Oh no! That stupid bird!" Bessy screeched as her stomach growled back at her.

Bessy's lunch was no longer plain nor ordinary. It was now quite extraordinary. While Bessy was chasing the bird around, she somehow managed to knock her sandwich off the table and onto the dirty floor. After she picked it up, she placed the top slice of bread back on top of the bologna that was now covered with dust, dirt, and other gross items from the carpet.

"Well, I'm not eating this," Bessy said as she shoved the unique delicacy back into her bag. Before she had a chance to get up from her stool, a homely looking fellow with an oval belly opened the door and trotted over to the table where Bessy was sitting. He was carrying a tray.

"Hey, lady. Here's your lunch." The man looked at Bessy's brown bag in a puzzled way. "What's in that bag?"

"It's supposed to be my lunch."

"Why you sneak! How dare you order your lunch! You think that you're too good for the cafeteria food? You're nothing special. Mr. Jacobs told me to bring you your lunch and here you sit like a pig chowing down fancy food. Why didn't you tell me you were too important to eat my cookin? I hate people like you. You step on us little people like we're slaves."

Bessy thought if the man insulting her was a little person, she would hate to meet a big person.

"Don't just sit there and give me that blank look," the man said. "Say something, library lady."

Bessy was star stunned. She couldn't believe that a man whom she had never met in her life could come in and give her such a raking when she hadn't done anything to him. He was as rude as Wartella Snollygoster. When Bessy had gathered her thoughts, she came up with a great plan. "I'm sorry if I did something wrong, sir," Bessy said. "Please forgive me. Mr. Jacobs didn't tell me you delivered. After all, I am new here."

"Oh, I guess I can forgive you this once, lady."

"I have an idea," Bessy said. "I feel so sorry for causing you all this extra trouble. Since you have been so kind to bring this good food all the way from the cafeteria, I'll eat it. It looks great."

"You don't have to."

"Oh, I insist. Just set that tray down here and I'll take care of the rest. I can't thank you enough, sir. You have gone to such great extremes to make my first day one I shall never forget. You deserve something special."

"It was nothing, lady."

"I insist on rewarding you, though, Mr. ...What's your name?"

"Steamy, lady. Hotand Steamy."

"Well, Mr. Steamy, tell me. Do you like bologna?"

"I adore it."

"I'm so glad you do. All heroes deserve rewards. Some get the Nobel Peace Prize, others maybe the Congressional Medal of Honor. And you, Mr. Hotand Steamy, deserve something too. Here. Take my bologna sandwich. I can't think of anybody who I would rather see eat it. And surely nobody deserves it more than you do."

"Are you sure, lady?"

"I'm certain. Here you go. I hope you enjoy it."

"Thanks a lot, lady. You're as nice as my friend Grace. She gave me a whole sack of cheeseburgers for picking up her ticket at the travel agency."

"Don't thank me. You earned it, sir."

"Goodbye, lady."

"Goodbye, Mr. Steamy."

As soon as Mr. Steamy had left the library, Bessy began laughing so hard that she fell off the stool she was sitting on. When she recovered, she sat back down and began devouring the lunch that Mr. Steamy had so kindly delivered to her. The school food turned out to be terrible. Bessy's belly, which had been growling all morning for some attention, was now begging for mercy. Bessy wondered if she would have been better off eating the bologna sandwich after she had eaten Mr. Steamy's food. Hopefully she would recover before <u>The Adventures of Huckleberry Finn</u> arrived.

Chapter 10

It had arrived! Bessy curiously watched as the truck carrying the original first copy of Mark Twain's <u>The Adventures of Huckleberry Finn</u> pulled up in front of the high school. The truck slowly came to a halt. Bessy could hardly believe it. The famous book was finally at the school. This was one of the most exciting moments in Bessy's life. She patiently waited for the metal door on the back of the truck to slide up so the book could be taken into the library. While she was waiting, Mr. Jacobs came out of the school and walked over towards her.

"It's finally here I see," he said.

"It sure is," Bessy said. "Isn't this exciting?"

"It really is, Bessy."

"I wonder what's taking so long?" Bessy asked.

"I suppose they're just being extra careful with the book so they don't damage it," Mr. Jacobs said.

The conversation was interrupted by a clicking sound. Suddenly, the door on the back of the truck slid up and down came a ramp. A thin, black-haired woman in a security suit came running down the ramp screaming at the top of her lungs. "Look out! Get out of the way, you morons! Get back or get a smack!" It was Jane Blab, Mr. Blab's daughter.

Bessy and Mr. Jacobs darted away from the yelling woman. "Who in the world is she?" Mr. Jacobs asked Bessy in a whisper.

"Oh, no. It looks like Jane Blab," Bessy said as she rubbed her eyes in disbelief.

Jane walked over towards Bessy and Mr. Jacobs. "Where's the principal?" Jane demanded.

"That's me," Mr. Jacobs said.

"I'm Jane Blab. I'll be helping you guard the book in the library. I'm the temporary worker the superintendent hired."

"Oh, well I'm glad to meet you," Mr. Jacobs said as he held out his hand to shake hers.

"Don't lie," Jane said as she walked back towards the truck. Then she turned around and walked back over towards Bessy and Mr. Jacobs. "Is that you, Bessy Beebody? What are you doing here? Did they hire a new janitor?"

"No they didn't," Bessy said. "I happen to be the librarian who's in charge of this book while it's here."

"I guess that means you're my boss for a while," Jane said with a devilish grin.

"That's right," Bessy said.

"Boss, smoss. You'd better be a darn good one. If you mess up at all, I'll be sure to tell Mr. Superintendent all about it," Jane said. Then she turned again and rudely walked back over to the truck. Mr. Jacobs and Bessy looked at each other. They were speechless. Bessy thought that Jane had become even more hateful and cocky than she used to be. The one thing that could happen to ruin what would have been a wonderful moment had happened.

Jane yelled up into the truck. "Hey! You two clowns! What are you doing? You're supposed to be delivering the book, not reading it! Hurry up!"

In a moment two men quietly came down the ramp carrying a big box. Jane opened the door, and the two men and the box that contained the famous book entered the school. Bessy and Mr. Jacobs followed behind them as they headed to the library, which was empty of people except for Bessy's student aide, Idunno. Jane, who was taking her security job too seriously, ran over to the boy. "Who are you?" Jane shouted.

"Idunno," he said as he shook with fear.

"Don't tell me you don't know. I bet you're planning on stealing this book," Jane said.

Bessy and Mr. Jacobs dashed over to where Jane had Idunno by the shirt collar. "Stop that!" Mr. Jacobs and Bessy said together.

"I'm not hurting this brat," Jane said as she released Idunno from her grasp. Idunno ran over into Bessy's arms and began crying.

"Mrs. Blab, you are not going to be allowed to carry on like this," Mr. Jacobs said. "I'm going to put you on suspension. I'll inform the superintendent how you've been behaving, and you can pick up what salary you've earned at the office."

"You can't do that!" Jane screamed.

"Oh yes I can," Mr. Jacobs said. "Please leave the school now."

"I'll fix you!" Jane threatened, much like the witch in <u>The Wizard of Oz</u>. "I'll fix all of you. I'll tell my daddy." Then she raced out of the library shouting. "This was all your fault, Bessy Beebody. We'll see how long you stay employed."

As soon as Jane left the library, everyone in the room felt happier. The delivery men went about their business while Mr. Jacobs talked with Bessy.

"I'm sorry about that," Mr. Jacobs said.

"That's all right," Bessy said. "I'm used to her. She never liked me since the day my cake recipe beat hers at the county fair."

"Are you O.K., Idunno?" the principal asked.

"Yes, sir," Idunno said.

"How about coming with me?" Mr. Jacobs said to the boy. "I'll get you a soda pop and you can rest in the office the rest of the day, if it's all right with Bessy." Idunno began to smile.

"Sure it's all right with me," Bessy said. "You take good care of my aide, though. I'll need him this week when all the people come in here to see this famous book."

"I'm going to talk to the superintendent and tell him all about this little incident," Mr. Jacobs said. "Don't worry about a thing, Bessy. I know you can take good care of the book by yourself. Let me or Grace know if you need anything. Just be certain to lock up before you leave today. The security case should keep the book safe." Then Mr. Jacobs and little Idunno left the library and headed to the office.

Chapter 11

Bessy watched as the two delivery men carefully placed Mark Twain's <u>The Adventures of Huckleberry Finn</u> inside a glass display case for all of Balloonsboro High to see. The Official Librarian felt unworthy to have such a masterpiece in her library. The men working with the security case, unlike Bessy, seemed to be less enthused about the great book.

"Can you believe they won last night?" the one asked his partner.

"Sure can't," the other said. "Everybody said they didn't have a chance."

"Shows ya what everybody knows, huh?"

"Sure does."

"Did that screw fit in the back?"

"Yeah, but it was a tight fit."

"I guess she's ready to go then," the one stated as he stood up and handed Bessy a key. "Here you go, mam."

"Thank you, sir," Bessy said. "Do you by any chance know much about Mark Twain?"

"Nope, mam. I don't think I ever met any Twains. I used to know a Mark Carter, though. Boy, was he a character. I'll never forget him. He stole my milk money everyday for a year when I was in third grade. What a bully."

"Sorry to hear that," Bessy said.

"Yep, old Mark Carter. I still remember how he used to eat all them fish eyes and things we'd cut up in science class. For only a quarter he'd do it too. He was something else. We just never knew what. But as for Mark Twain, I don't think I knew him. What year did he graduate?"

Bessy was sorry she'd asked the man a question. It was pretty obvious that the only Twain this man might know was a choo choo twain. "Mark Twain isn't from around here," Bessy explained. "He's a famous writer."

"Oh, that's neat. He's a rider!" the other man said as he joined the conversation. "I always did like rodeos. How long has he been riding anyway?"

Bessy shook her head in disbelief. Her ears turned red and began to quiver. She felt like she could grow horns and blow smoke. She would have done it too, but her hair was already messed up enough without horns, and as for blowing smoke, that certainly was not anything for a health conscious librarian to do. "Not riding. Writing. Like writing books. Mark Twain is one of the greatest American novelists there's ever been."

"That is neat," the rodeo fan said. "You mean he's a writer and a novelist too. I bet having two jobs keeps him busy."

Bessy felt a horn beginning to sprout and sensed smoke leaving her already red ears. "He doesn't write anymore," she said. "He's dead."

"Ain't it a shame," Mark Carter's acquaintance said, "I guess two jobs will do that to a person."

"Yeah, I guess so," Bessy agreed, hoping that the two men would soon be leaving. "Thank you for installing the security case for us, gentlemen."

"You're welcome, mam," rodeo dude's sidekick said. "We'll give this other key to Mr. Jacobs. You and him are the only ones with keys to the security alarm. Mr. Lender said that you were to get the book out only if there was a fire or something like that. The alarm is already on, so unless you stick a key in, it'll go off if you try to open the case. If you have any problems, Mr. Lender said to call the office."

"We sure will," Bessy said.

"Have a nice day, mam," the one man said while the other put a stick of gum in his mouth.

"Thank you," Bessy replied, and the two men left the library. Bessy glanced at the great book. She read the title aloud, "The Adventures of Huckleberry Finn." It was an awesome spectacle. Bessy felt a burst of joy go down her back.

"Hi, Bessy."

"Who said that?" Bessy asked.

"I did."

Bessy looked around and said, "Who's talking?" Nobody else was in the room.

"Me!"

"All right, Me, where are you?"

"In here."

Bessy looked inside the glass case. It was the book. "Oh surely not," Bessy said. "This can't be happening."

"It is, though," the book said.

"You're a book, and books don't talk."

"Who said so?"

"Well, I don't know. It just doesn't make any..."

"Any booksense?" the book said.

"I suppose you might say that. But you can't. I mean books don't talk."

"Maybe you just don't listen. Have you ever tried to talk to a book before, Bessy?"

"No. I haven't. But that's beside the point... And how do you know my name?" Bessy asked.

"I heard the literacy workers at the museum say that I'd be going to Bessy Beebody's library in Balloonsboro first, and this is my first stop if I'm not mistaken."

"No, Mr. Book, you're quite correct."

"Please, Bessy, there's no need for formalities. Feel free to call me THE."

"Why should I call you THE?"

"It's my first name, isn't it? Just like my last name is FINN and my middle name is ADVENTURESOFHUCKLEBERRY."

"O.K. then, THE. Let me be the first to welcome you to the Balloonsboro High School Library."

"The pleasure is mine."

"Is there anything I can do for you, THE?" Bessy asked her new guest.

"It is a little stuffy in here. What about opening this sardine can for a minute. It'll give you and me a better chance to see each other up close too."

"I don't know if I should," Bessy said. I could get into a lot of trouble. I'd feel just awful if something happened to you."

"Don't be such a fraidy cat. It's not like I have legs to run off somewhere. Who do you think I am? The little gingerbread man?"

"You don't have a mouth either, but you're talking to me."

"That's only because you're special, Bessy. Only a few literate people in the world ever read enough to understand Booklish."

"What's Booklish?" Bessy asked.

"Booklish is the language of all books. It's like English, only with a Book instead of an Eng. Booklish is what books use to communicate with each other."

"That's neat. You mean you books actually have your own language?"

"If I'm not telling the truth then <u>Gone with the Wind</u> is a comic book."

"That's just super neat, THE."

"It's just something most people don't know about."

"So if you have your own language then you must have things like families."

"Of course we do. Your Brady Bunch is like our Encyclopedias."

"That's amazing."

"I'm glad you find it so interesting. Let me out of here for a bit and I'll tell you some more. This heat won't help my pages a bit."

Bessy quickly used her key to turn off the alarm. She lifted the case and carefully picked up THE.

"Boy your hands are sweaty, Bessy," the book said.

"Oh, I'm sorry."

"Don't be sorry. I was a little thirsty anyway."

"You mean you drink sweat?"

"What else am I supposed to drink? Air? When's the last time you saw a water fountain for books?"

"I never thought of it like that before."

"That's the way most people are nowadays. They forget that we books were once trees. Sure, I might not sprout leaves anymore, but I still like an occasional sip of water. It's sort of like your drunks and their liquor. We books can't break the habit either."

"You really are a lot like a person, THE."

"All of us are very similar to people. We even have spines."

"That's true," Bessy agreed.

"Our ancestry even parallels yours, Bessy."

"Really?"

"Really. You know how all of your relatives came from Adam? Well, mine all came from some of the first trees he used to make paper with to write on."

"You mean Adam knew how to write?"

"Of course he did. Just because he was first doesn't mean he was a dummy."

"I guess that's true. I'm going to put you down for a minute."

"O.K., Bessy. Just lay me on your desk."

Bessy slowly walked to her desk and placed the expensive book on her desktop. "There you go, THE. Is there anything else I can do for you?"

"Well, do you see that cute little paperback copy of <u>The Best Christmas Pageant Ever</u>?"

"Yes."

"Could you bring her over and give us a chance to get to know each other?"

"I take it you're not married."

"That's right. I never did find anybody who had a tone to suit me."

"So you books have relationships?"

"Of course. All books have gender in case you're wondering. Our gender is determined by our author. If our author is male then so are we, and if our author is female then we are too. When we have more than one author, we go by the first author's gender."

"Do you books have any idea of death?"

"We most certainly do. All books are born when they're written and printed. After that we live until we start falling apart. That's why I'm so anxious to get hitched. I'm no spring chicken."

"Let me get her for you," Bessy said as she walked over and got the book THE wanted to see. "Hey, she's got the same first name you do. Isn't that confusing?"

"We books go by the second word if there's a word like a, an, or the at the beginning of someone's name. To me she's BEST. I just said you could call me THE so I wouldn't confuse you. Besides, THE is a lot easier than saying ADVENTURES. My close friends call me Ad."

"I understand," Bessy said, as she placed the supposedly cute paperback next to THE on the library desk. "Here she is. I'll let you two talk for a minute while I see what's going on outside."

Chapter 12

Bessy thought she heard someone coming. She quickly walked over to her desk where <u>The Adventures of Huckleberry Finn</u> was talking with <u>The Best Christmas Pageant Ever</u>. Bessy quickly picked up THE and then rushed over to his glass case.

"Hey! What's the problem?" the famous book asked.

"If someone comes in here and sees that I've taken you out of your security case, I might lose my job," Bessy said.

"Oh, Bessy. You worry too much. Besides, I didn't even hear anything."

"Maybe you didn't, but I'm not going to take any chances."

"I was just getting to know <u>The Best Christmas Pageant Ever</u>, though," the book said. "She thinks I'm cute."

"Well, I'm sorry to spoil your picnic, but if someone came in here while you were out, I'd get in big trouble," Bessy said as she lifted the glass security case up and gently placed the book back on the soft red cloth he had been lying on. "There you go. You just rest up now."

"What else am I going to do in this prison?" the unhappy book stated.

"Oh, THE. I wish you wouldn't have that kind of an attitude."

"Well, I do. How would you like to be kept in a glass case like an animal all of your life?"

"I wouldn't," Bessy said.

"Of course you wouldn't. How do you think I feel?"

"What can I do about it, though?" Bessy asked. "I'm just an Official Librarian."

"Oh, I wish I could cry and mildew to death," the book said.

"Don't talk like that, THE. Stop it right now. If you relax and behave yourself, I'll make a deal with you."

"What kind of a deal?"

"If you promise to be a good book, I'll take you home with me tonight."

"Do you really mean it, Bessy?"

"Only if you keep your half of the bargain, though. Do you promise to cheer up?"

"I sure do," the book said.

"All right then, as soon as school's out today, you and I are going home."

"Hurray!" the book shouted.

"Not so loud," Bessy said. "Someone might hear you."

"No they won't. Remember. Only a few real smart people like you can hear and understand Booklish."

"Oh, I forgot about that. Well then... Cheer all you like. I'd better get back to work." With these words Bessy Beebody gracefully walked back over to her desk and began to make out a list of students who had overdue books. Being an Official Librarian wasn't easy.

Chapter 13

L ater in the afternoon Bessy decided to examine the audio-visual equipment. An Official Librarian by no means just worked with books alone. Bessy was also responsible for record players, VCRs, cassettes, cassette players, film projectors, records, video tapes and so on. When Bessy discovered that most of the equipment was in terrible shape, she became very upset.

"This is awful!" Bessy said. "I never saw stuff in such a bad condition."

To a normal person the equipment was just old and unserviced, but through the eyes of an Official Librarian, all of the audio-visual objects were alive and possessed human characteristics. Bessy went right to work. She replaced knobs, wrapped up cords, dusted carts, and focused lenses. One record player had a dreadful problem. It was so old that whenever it was turned on it squeaked like a mouse with hot coals in his britches. Bessy had respect for the elderly, especially for record players. After all, they received no social security and somebody had to take care of them. Bessy applied some of Slimy Sam's Super Duper Lubricant to the helpless record player like she was feeding a baby. When the record player was finished nursing,

Bessy moved on to the next appliance. It was a dark green film projector.

"Just look at you, fellow," Bessy said. "You're a 1962 Hudson. You're an antique." Bessy was amazed with the film projector's appearance. Although the rest of the equipment had been beaten up and mistreated, the priceless projector seemed to be in perfect shape. Bessy excitedly plugged the projector's cord into a nearby electrical outlet and flipped the power switch on.

PRESTO!

The projector produced a glorious stream of brilliant light upon the dingy wall. Bessy went back to her youth and began to create shadow animals with her hands and the wonderful projector's assistance. Bessy was exceptionally good at this type of art. First she made a bird, then a rabbit. Next was a butterfly, then an alligator, and the list went on to include just about every creature that ever stepped aboard Noah's Ark. Bessy's hands fluttered and flapped as fast as her bird visitor's wings had during lunch that day. Things were going great in Bessy Beebody's life. She was having a preview of Official Librarian's Heaven. It wasn't meant to last, though.

PING!

Without warning, the projector's light bulb went out and canceled Bessy's show.

"Well, I'll be dogged," Bessy said. "Now I'm going to have to locate some spare bulbs."

Bessy searched in every nook and cranny throughout the library until she finally came across a whole sack of replacement bulbs that ranged in size from teeny-tiny to massively monstrous. Balloonsboro's Bessy Beebody was back in business, or so it appeared that she was. Bessy carefully studied the precious machine she had to perform the procedure on, after locating the correct sized replacement bulb. Then she began to change the bulb. Bessy opened a little metal door and carefully squeezed her hand inside. Once inside, her fingers patiently unscrewed the old bulb and pulled it out of the socket it was in. Bessy then began to remove her hand and the old bulb. Something was wrong, though. Bessy's hand was stuck inside the projector. She wiggled it one way and then the other, but it did no good.

"Darn, Darn, Darn!" Bessy cried. "What am I going to do now?"

Bessy moved her hand in directions that she never knew she could. Still, her hand was trapped inside the machine like a mouse in a trap. After Bessy had struggled with the projector for half an hour and was still connected to it, she felt that it was time to get help. She was far too proud to tell someone in school about what had happened. They would make her the laughing stock of the town if they ever found out about her predicament. Since it was almost three o'clock, Bessy decided to leave a little early and solve her problem out of school.

As she turned the lights off and locked the library doors, her stomach began to feel upset. Bessy rushed outside to her red station wagon with the film projector still hanging on the end of her arm like an oversized baseball glove. On the way out of the building, Bessy tripped on the projector's cord several times. From a distance, she looked like an uncoordinated space monster with a thin tail. Eventually, Bessy and her unhappy hand made it to the car. Bessy's bottom plunged down behind the steering wheel after she opened the car door. Then she started the engine and slammed the door, catching the projector's cord.

"Shoot fire!" Bessy shouted as she opened the door again and yanked the cord inside. She shut the door once more and began to drive onto the main road. Bessy decided to go to the hospital. She didn't think the police could do much for her, and she had already bothered the fire department once that day.

"I'm sure the hospital has some kind of a special tool to get this thing off my hand," Bessy said as she drove down the road. "I bet this sort of thing happens all the time."

Chapter 14

Bessy's drive to the hospital was a terrible experience. Since her right arm was attached to the film projector, she was forced to drive with only one hand. To make matters worse, she began sneezing like a baby in a pepper factory. Nevertheless, she eventually arrived at the Balloonsboro Memorial Hospital. After she drove up to the emergency entrance, she slammed on the brakes and sighed. "Thank goodness I made it," Bessy said.

Suddenly, the emergency room doors burst open, and two attendants raced out with a stretcher to Bessy's car and opened her door. "What's wrong, mam? Have you been shot?" one attendant asked.

"Why no, sir."

"Did you take an overdose?"

"Nope."

"Oh my. Then you must be having a baby! Don't you worry, mam. We'll take good care of you." Bessy couldn't get a word in edgewise. The one talkative attendant must've been related to Mr. Blab. Within seconds, Bessy found herself strapped down on a stretcher in the delivery room. Neither attendant had seemed to notice that Bessy's right hand was stuck in a film projector. They just dropped her off like mailmen and left. "Somebody help me!" Bessy shouted.

A short, filled-out nurse stepped into the room where Bessy was confined. "I know it hurts, honey, but you know what they say. No pain, no gain."

"You don't understand," Bessy explained. "I'm not having a baby."

"Well, if you aren't having a baby, what are you doing here?"

"It's really not my fault. Two lunatics brought me here and tied me down before I had a chance to tell them what was wrong."

"What's wrong then, honey?"

"If you'll look at my hand you'll see. I've managed to get my hand caught in this film projector when I was changing the light bulb."

"Oh my!" the nurse said with a smile. "How did you ever get that stuck on your arm? You must be pretty stupid. I had an uncle who used to do ignorant things like this all the time."

"If you don't mind, I'd like to get out of here as soon as I can," Bessy said.

"Sure, hun. Let me get you transported and try to locate a doctor."

In about seven minutes, Bessy was in an operating room. She had never been so scared, angry, and embarrassed in all her life. Mr. Humiliation seemed to have Bessy's hand in a vise. Bessy wondered if she would be able to get out of the hospital without getting her hand amputated. The operating room was as cold as a meatlocker. Bessy felt icicles forming on her ears and inside her fireboots on the ends of her toes.

"Sure is chilly in here, isn't it?" someone said to Bessy.

Bessy looked around. Nobody was there. It had been a rough day. Bessy figured her mind was playing tricks on her.

"I say, isn't it a bit cool in here today?"

"Who's talking?" Bessy asked as she looked all around for a person.

"It is I. Hudson, the 1962 film projector."

"Oh no. Don't tell me you talk too," Bessy said.

"I most certainly do."

"I suppose you speak Projectorlish?"

"How'd you know?"

"Just a lucky guess."

"Since we're sorta linked up at the moment, how about dropping the formal titles? I'll call you Bessy, and you can feel free to call me Huddy."

"Sounds like an O.K. deal to me."

"Good. Then it's settled."

"I hope I haven't hurt you, Huddy. All I wanted to do was change your bulb."

"I realize that, Bessy. Accidents happen. Don't worry about it."

"Thanks, Huddy. You're awfully understanding."

"I try to be. Sometimes I admit it's hard, though."

"Why haven't you ever said anything to me before?"

"This is the first chance I've really had. I'd never met you until today, and before we got to this ice box I was taking a nap."

"Oh, I see. So you appliances sleep?"

"That's right. And why shouldn't we? Don't you like a good snoozer every so often?"

"Of course I do. It's a must for people I know. Hey, listen. Someone's coming."

A doctor wearing glasses entered the cold room. He was reading Bessy's chart, or something on a clipboard which he was holding in his left hand. "How are you today, Bessy? My name is Dr. Young and I'm a pediatrician." When the doctor looked at Bessy's terrible looking outfit, his jaw dropped open. "Oh my gosh! What happened to your clothes? Were you in a wreck? They didn't tell me?"

"I'm just fine," Bessy said. "The problem is this thing on my hand."

"Boy you must be pretty stupid to get your hand caught in a ... Oh my goodness sakes alive!" the doctor said.

"What's wrong!" Bessy yelled in horror.

"Your hand's caught in a 1962 Hudson. You see, I collect audio-visual equipment. Obviously you are closer to your collection than I am to mine. Ha ha ha!"

"That was a pretty good one, Bessy? Wasn't it?" Huddy said.

"Oh be quiet before I break your lens!" Bessy said.

The doctor backed off and put his glasses in his coat pocket. "There's no need to be violent, Bessy," the doctor said.

"I wasn't talking to you, doctor."

"Oh, all right then. Whatever you say."

"He thinks you're crazy now, Bessy," the projector said.

"Why don't you just shut up! Please," Bessy said.

"All right, Bessy," the doctor said. "If you don't want to talk then I'll just go straight to work and try to keep quiet."

Bessy didn't even attempt to explain to the doctor that she was talking to the film projector. She wasn't about to get sent to the mental hospital by a baby doctor. One hospital a day was enough for her. Dr. Young finally managed to free Bessy's hand from Huddy's mouth. The young doctor was even kind enough to change the projector's light bulb at no extra cost. Bessy was happy to get home that day. After she had read Huddy a story and said her prayers, she sluggishly hopped into bed and immediately fell asleep. Her first day was downright exhausting.

It was midnight when Bessy woke up in a cold sweat. "Oh no!" she said. "I forgot all about poor THE. I promised him I'd bring him home with me tonight." Bessy didn't think twice about the matter. She knew what had to be done. She abruptly got dressed and ran out to her car carrying Huddy by the handle. Hopefully he could help explain Bessy's projector predicament to THE so he wouldn't hold a grudge. Once in the car, Bessy and Huddy drove towards the school.

Chapter 15

W hen Bessy pulled up in front of Balloonsboro High's side door, she had no trouble finding a parking space. The morning darkness was broken in spots by the high school's security lights. After she parked, Bessy got out of her station wagon and walked over to the school door. She was carrying Huddy by his handle. Once inside, Bessy raced down the hallway towards the library.

"What's going on!" Huddy asked.

"I'm sorry," Bessy said. "I didn't mean to wake you up."

"How could anybody sleep when somebody's holding them by the handle and jerking them all over the place? Where are we anyway? It looks like the school?"

"You're right. It is the school. I'm sorry to wake you up, but I didn't want to come out this late all by myself."

"I'm glad I make you feel safe, Bessy, but what am I supposed to do if we run into trouble?"

"Beats me. Maybe if we should meet a mugger or something you could shine your light in his eyes. You do have a new light bulb now."

"Sounds like a good idea to me. It would help if I was plugged in, though."

"Why don't you just be quiet for a minute? I'm too busy worrying about what THE is going to say to me after I broke my promise to him. I don't need any smart aleck remarks from you right now."

"I didn't ask to come along, you know."

"I know. Just try to relax and go back to sleep."

"I thought you wanted company."

"I changed my mind," Bessy said as she entered the library after unlocking the door. Bessy turned the lights on and looked over at the glass display case where she had last spoken with The Adventures of Huckleberry Finn. The case had been opened and was now empty. THE was gone!

"Oh no!" Bessy cried. "Where's THE?"

"Don't ask me," Huddy said. "You told me to be quiet."

"This is terrible. What in the world could have happened to poor THE?"

"Looks like somebody stole him. Think it was a mugger? Maybe you'd better plug me in so I can shine my light in his eyes."

"This is serious, Huddy. If THE's gone, I might lose my job."

"Don't worry about it, Bessy. You won't need it where you're going."

"What do you mean?"

"How could you work while you're in jail for stealing a famous book like THE. I bet he was worth a lot of money."

"I didn't steal THE, though. You know I didn't."

"Tell that to the police."

"Boy are you a big help. I should have let that doctor at the hospital keep you."

"At least he knows how to change my light bulb without getting his hand caught inside of me."

"I'm not going to stand here and argue with you. I guess I'd better call the police."

"Why don't you call the principal first?"

"I better call the police first. That way when Mr. Jacobs finds out about what I've let happen, they'll be here when he tries to strangle me."

"Don't worry about Mr. Jacobs."

"Why shouldn't I?"

"I can shine my light in his eyes while you run away. Remember?"

"This is no time to joke," Bessy said as she sat Huddy down on her desk. "I'm going to look around in the library and see if THE's still in here. You sit there and try to figure out what's happened to him."

"Who do you think I am? Sherlock Holmes?"

"Of course not. You're Watson. Now be quiet and think."

Bessy searched all over the library for THE. He was nowhere to be seen.

"Now who would have stolen poor, helpless THE?" Bessy said.

"I don't know," Huddy said. "Who do you think could have stolen him?"

"I really don't know."

"Why didn't the alarm go off? I thought it was supposed to protect THE from vandals."

"It was, but I forgot to turn the alarm back on when I put THE back in his case today."

"You mean you took him out of his case?"

"I'm afraid I did."

"This doesn't look good, Bessy. I hope you have a good lawyer."

"Thanks for the encouragement."

"No problem."

"Did you think of any brilliant plan to find THE while I was looking for him?"

"Not really. I do have an idea, though. Maybe we really can be like Sherlock Holmes and Watson.

"What do you mean?" Bessy asked.

"I figure that if we work together, we can locate THE. With me talking to the other electrical equipment, and you checking out the human suspects, we're certain to find him."

"That's a great idea, Huddy. Let's not waste a minute. Maybe we can find THE before Mr. Jacobs finds out he was stolen."

Chapter 16

"I suppose we should try to find some clues," Bessy said.

"Sounds like a good idea to me. Do you see any?" Huddy asked.

"I don't guess I do. Do you?"

"I'm not sure if it's a clue or not, but isn't that window over there open?"

"Well, I'll be... It is, isn't it?" Bessy cautiously walked over to the window.

"Do you see anything unusual?" Huddy asked as Bessy examined the window.

"No. I don't see... Oh my! Look at this!"

"What is it, Bessy?"

"It looks like a piece of black hair. It was caught in the hinge." Bessy shut the window. "I wonder who it belongs to."

"If you find that out, I bet you'll know who the villain is," Huddy said.

"Whoever was in here had to come from the courtyard outside because the library doors weren't opened since I left this afternoon."

"So it's probably a faculty member."

"Maybe, but maybe not. Someone else may have used one of the other school employee's keys without him or her knowing about it."

"I guess that's possible."

"If only this window had been locked, I might not be in such a mess right now."

"That window used to have a lock. I remember seeing it last spring when they had me out here showing a film to one of the classes."

"I wonder what happened to it."

"I bet it's in the back room with all the other films."

"Not the film, silly. I'm talking about the lock. I wonder how long its been gone."

"Just leave it to me. I think I can find out. Could you hold me up to that speaker on the wall over there?"

"I sure will. Hurry up, though. You're heavy." Bessy picked Huddy up off her desk and lifted him over her head, after she walked over towards a brown speaker that was attached to the wall.

"Excuse me!" Huddy said.

"Wha wha wha what's going on here? Is there a fire?" the speaker asked in a groggy voice.

"No, there's no fire, sir," Huddy said.

"What's the problem then?"

"Sorry to bother you, Mr. Speaker, but my friend Bessy has gotten herself in a bit of a mess."

"What kind of a mess?"

"Well, you see, Bessy was in charge of a book that was in that glass case over there, and it seems to have been stolen. We were looking for clues and happened to notice that the window over there was open."

"So what. Haven't you ever seen a window open before?"

"Of course I have, but we were wondering what happened to the lock. I told Bessy that I thought that window had a lock last spring, but I haven't been out of the audio-visual room since then. We thought, since you're always out in this part of the library, you might have noticed what happened to the lock."

"Let me think a minute," the speaker said with a yawn.

"Hurry up, Huddy. You're heavy," Bessy said.

"I'm hurrying," the projector replied. "Mr. Speaker, could you please think a little faster. My friend's arms aren't real strong."

"Certainly. What was the question again?" the speaker asked.

"When was the lock taken off the window?" Huddy asked.

"What window?"

"The one over there in this room."

"Oh, yeah. I believe, if I remember correctly, that lock was removed last week."

"That's great. Do you remember who removed the lock by any chance?" Huddy asked.

"What lock?"

"You know! The lock on the window over there."

"Nope, I'm sorry. I think I must've been asleep. I just recall it was there up until last week."

"Thanks for your time, sir."

"That's all right. I'm glad you woke me up. I had the scariest dream earlier tonight. I dreamt that I was in here at night and a big, black, hairy animal was messing around with stuff. I've never had such a realistic dream in my life."

"Sorry to hear about that. I guess I better go now. Bessy's arms are getting tired. Thanks again."

"Don't mention it. See ya later."

"Down, Bessy," Huddy said.

"It's about time," Bessy said as she lowered the projector and carried him over to her desk where she sat him down. "Did you find anything out?"

"Couldn't you hear us talking?"

"No, I couldn't."

"That's odd. I was speaking to him in Electricappliancelish, though. I guess you only know Aristocratic Booklish and Projectorlish."

"What's that mean, in English?" Bessy asked.

"It means that you can only understand older books and appliances when they talk."

"Oh. So tell me what the speaker had to say for himself."

"He said that the lock had been removed from the window sometime last week."

"That's great. So the culprit must have planned this whole scheme to steal poor THE even before I began working here. The villain was expecting the book to arrive here this week."

"That really doesn't help much, Bessy. The whole town knew the book was going to arrive this week. Didn't it?"

"I suppose you're right. Anybody could have done it."

"Anybody with black hair and a lock."

"Whoever it was had to leave a trail. Let's go outside and see if we can find any footprints."

Chapter 17

Plop! Bessy's feet landed on the ground. She and Huddy had successfully managed to climb out the library window.

"See anything unusual, Huddy?" Bessy asked.

"What's that by your foot, Bessy?"

Bessy bent down and picked something up with her fingers. "It's another piece of that black hair. We must be on the right track."

"I sure hope so," Huddy said.

"Look here!" Bessy said.

"What is it?"

"It's a great big footprint."

"Oh good. Now we can tell what kind of shoes the book thief was wearing."

"I don't think so, Huddy."

"Why not?"

"The guy who made these tracks wasn't wearing any shoes."

"Are you serious?"

"Yep. I sure am. He was definitely barefoot. Look for yourself."

Huddy studied the prints as Bessy held him close to the ground. "Golly," Huddy said. "They're gigantic. If he ever stubbed his toe, he'd have to call a tow truck."

"Who could have made such large tracks?" Bessy asked.

"Maybe we should ask what instead of who. What if these tracks belong to some monster or something?" Huddy asked.

"Don't be silly, Huddy. Everybody knows there's no such thing as monsters."

"I hope you're right, Bessy."

"Quit talking silly. Let's follow these tracks and try to find THE."

Bessy, still holding Huddy by his handle, slowly followed the giant footprints from the library window all the way across the courtyard in the middle of the school. Every so often a piece of black hair could be seen along the trail. The trail led Bessy and Huddy straight to the vice-principal's office window.

"What do you think about this?" Huddy asked his partner.

"I can hardly believe that the vice-principal would be involved in this. Let's see what's inside. Luckily this window doesn't have a lock on it either." Bessy pushed the window open and quietly climbed into the vice-principal's office, still firmly holding onto Huddy's handle.

"Boy it's dark in here, Bessy," Huddy said.

"I'll try to find the light switch," Bessy said. "Hold on a minute." Bessy felt her way around the office until she found the switch and turned the lights on. "Isn't that better now?" Bessy asked her friend.

"I suppose so. Hey, look over there. It's a gorilla suit."

"Now things are beginning to make sense. That's the same gorilla suit Harold Harpelander was wearing when he scared me. He must be the book thief."

"I bet you're right, Bessy. This makes sense now. The speaker in the library told me that he had a bad dream where a black haired animal was in the library. I bet he saw the vice-principal stealing THE."

"I bet you're right. Here's a piece of the furry hair I found caught in the window. Does it match Harold's costume, Huddy?" Bessy asked as she held the piece of black fur up to the vice-principal's costume.

"It looks like the hair on the costume is a lighter shade of black. That's odd," Huddy said.

"You're right. It should match," Bessy said.

"Why don't you put the gorilla suit on and we can go back outside and see if the footprints out there match the costume's footprints."

"That's a good idea, Huddy. I'll sit you down on the floor for a minute while I put this thing on."

In a couple of minutes, Bessy had squeezed into the gorilla suit. "How do I look?" Bessy asked.

"Much better," Huddy said.

"You ought to be a comedian. Come on now. Let's go back outside." With these words Bessy the gorilla picked up Huddy and went back to the courtyard.

Chapter 18

As Bessy hopped down from the vice-principal's office window, lightning bugs helped the security lights illuminate the courtyard area.

"Here we go again," Bessy said after she and Huddy had landed on the ground. "Let's go out in the middle where there's more light so we can compare footprints easier."

"Whatever you say, Bessy. I'm not about to argue with a mean gorilla like you," said Huddy.

"That's good. Maybe I should wear this monkey suit all the time. I bet I'd get more respect than other librarians."

"I bet so too."

Bessy reached the center of the courtyard and located one of the mysterious footprints. "How should I do this?" Bessy asked.

"Just put your foot down right beside that footprint and press down real hard," Huddy said.

"Is this good enough?" Bessy asked after she had followed her friend's instructions.

"Yeah. That looks just fine. Now slowly lift your foot up and let's compare the prints," Huddy said. Bessy slowly lifted her foot. She had made a beautiful gorilla footprint. "You did a good job, Bessy," Huddy said.

"Thanks," Bessy replied. "Do they match up?"

Huddy closely examined the prints. "They sure don't," Huddy said. "Compared to the print you just made, that other print would have to belong to something or someone much bigger than the gorilla suit owner."

"Who or what could make such a big print?" Bessy asked.

"I'm not sure, but I bet that whoever or whatever made these tracks has a hard time finding a new pair of tennis shoes."

"At least we know that the vice-principal is probably innocent now," Bessy said.

"That's right."

"Who would have such a big foot and shed black, furry hair, though?" Bessy asked.

"Maybe it could have been him," Huddy said as he pointed his lens to Bessy's right. Bessy cautiously turned her head to see what Huddy was pointing at. There next to Bessy's side stood a giant, black, furry panther with sharp white teeth.

"Could be," Bessy said as she quickly collected her thoughts and ran with all her might towards the library window with Huddy in her hand.

Chapter 19

B essy quickly pushed the library window shut after climbing inside and leaned up against it with her body as she tried to catch her breath. Her hand was still clinging tight to Huddy's handle.

"Are you all right, Bessy?" Huddy asked.

"I think so."

"I thought you said there weren't any monsters."

"I did. I didn't say anything about giant black panthers, though."

"Why don't you look out the window and see if he's still there?" Huddy said.

"Why don't you?" Bessy said.

"You're the one in charge of the library. Not me."

"O.K. I'll look." Bessy quickly turned her head and peeked out the window with one eye open and the other one shut. "Don't see anything," she said as she turned back around and looked down at Huddy. "It must've been our imagination. It's awfully dark out tonight."

"You might have a real active imagination, but I know for certain that I saw that thing. Mr. Panther is real," Huddy said.

"I can hardly believe a giant panther is running around school," Bessy said. "I'm a grown woman. I don't have time to be chased by wild animals when poor THE is lost."

Tap! Tap! Tap!

"What's that?" Bessy asked Huddy.

"I think our imagination is tapping on the window with his claws," Huddy said.

Bessy turned and looked out the window. It was the giant panther trying to get inside. Bessy used the window curtain cord to tie the window handle to a large statue of an Indian that someone in the art class had made. The panther snarled and jumped up and down when it saw what Bessy had so cleverly done.

"That ought to keep him out," Bessy said.

"I sure hope so," Huddy said. "Now what do we do?"

"I think we need to get out of here," Bessy said as she picked Huddy back up again and left the library after she locked the doors. Bessy ran to the parking lot, jumped into her car, and took off.

"Where are we going?" Huddy asked.

"I'm not sure," Bessy said.

"Do you think that the giant panther stole THE?"

"I don't know, Huddy."

"Who do you think stole him then?"

"I don't know that either. It could've been a number of people. Jane Blab or Wartella Snollygoster might do something like this to get me fired. It could've even been Mr. Steamy if he found out I gave him a bologna sandwich that I dropped on the floor. I think I need to talk to a human. Let me see if Grace Dover is at home. She gave me her address in the office today."

"Don't you think I'm good enough to help?" Huddy asked as he and Bessy rode down Maple Street.

"Of course you are, Huddy. It's just that Grace has a shoulder I can cry on and you don't."

"Oh," Huddy said.

After they had passed a white house with 107 posted above the porch and a yellow house with 108 painted on the steps, Bessy and her film projector friend pulled up in front of a little brown house with Dover painted on the mailbox. "You wait here," Bessy said as she got out of the car and shut the door. Huddy took a nap while Bessy walked up to the door and rang the doorbell several times. Nobody answered. Bessy came back to the car and Huddy woke up.

"What did she say?" Huddy asked.

"Nobody came to the door," Bessy said.

"What now, Sherlock?"

"I think I'd like to go see if Mr. Jacobs is home. He's gotta find out about the book sooner or later. And if there's a giant panther in his school, he should probably know about it."

"He'll think you're crazy, Bessy."

"Because I saw a giant panther?"

"Yes. And also because you're still wearing that gorilla suit."

"Well, I completely forgot all about this costume after I saw Mr. Panther. I can take it off," Bessy said as she tried to unzip the gorilla suit zipper. It was stuck. "I can't get this zipper undone."

"I guess you'll have to keep it on then," Huddy said.

"This is ridiculous. Here I am at one thirty in the morning wearing a gorilla suit with a talking film projector. The original copy of <u>The Adventures of Huckleberry Finn</u> is lost, my job is at stake, and a giant black panther is chasing me around the school so I can't look for the book. I thought yesterday was the worst day of my life."

"I guess you were wrong," Huddy said. "I think today is."

"Huddy. I'm not about to lose this job. Being the Official Librarian of Balloonsboro High means too much to me. And I'm not about to let some black fur ball with fangs keep me from finding THE. We're going back!" Bessy said as she stepped on the accelerator and headed back to the school.

Chapter 20

Bessy and Huddy pulled back into the high school parking lot. As they got out of her red station wagon, the wind made a moaning noise in the trees. Bessy and Huddy slowly entered the school again and walked to the library. After Bessy unlocked the doors, she walked over to her desk and grabbed something out of her bottom drawer. It was a flashlight and a small leather bag.

"We might need these," Bessy said.

"Good thinking," Huddy said as his friend stuck the flashlight and the bag in her back pocket.

"Let's go," Bessy said.

Chapter 21

B essy and Huddy crept through the school's main hallway with only the security lights showing the way. They stopped at the principal's office where they found the door open. The two quietly stepped inside. Bessy pulled her flashlight out and turned it on. She scanned the room to make sure Mr. Panther wasn't in it.

"It looks safe," Bessy said.

"Let's check the place out," Huddy said.

"That's what I plan on doing," Bessy said. She put Huddy down on the secretary's desk.

"What's that wad of paper on the floor?" Huddy said. Bessy picked up the wad of paper, opened it, and shined the light on it. It read:

Dear Sirs,
We will be needing an extra security key for the book security case. Please send it to 109 Ma

"That's interesting," Bessy said. "It isn't finished. Whoever wrote this must've messed up and intended to throw this away. I guess it fell out of the trash can."

"I wonder what 109 Ma is?" Huddy asked.

"I'm not sure. I think we'll keep this, though." Bessy put the paper in her pocket and walked over to the filing cabinet. She opened it and flipped through the files.

"What are you looking for now?" Huddy asked.

"I'm trying to see which room is Wartella Snollygoster's so we can look for clues in it. She is a good suspect considering how much she dislikes me. Here it is. Room 109. That's not far from here."

"109," Huddy said. "That's the same number that was in that letter. Think there's a connection?"

"There very well might be," Bessy said. "You wait here while I go and take a look in Mr. Jacobs' office. Then we can go and check out old Snolly."

In a few minutes Bessy returned. "Did you find anything?" Huddy asked.

"Not a thing," Bessy said. "I guess we can go to Snolly's lair now."

"Isn't this a funny desk calendar?" Huddy said as Bessy picked him back up. Bessy looked at it. The calendar had a picture of a dog driving a car on it.

"Yeah, it is funny. We've got more important things to do right now besides looking at funny pictures, though," Bessy said as she stepped out into the hall and turned her flashlight off. "109 should be down this..."

Rarrrrr!

Bessy looked behind her. It was the giant panther. Bessy pulled the leather bag out of her pocket and emptied it on the floor. Marbles fell everywhere. Bessy and Huddy then took off down the hall while the panther stumbled on the marbles and fell down. Bessy ran all the way to the school kitchen holding Huddy by the handle.

"Do you think we lost him?" Huddy asked.

"I sure hope so," Bessy said. "I'm all out of marbles."

"Let me see if that can opener over there knows anything. Could you set me down by her?"

"Sure, Huddy. Hurry up, though. Old fang face might come in here any minute." Bessy placed Huddy down by an electric can opener that was sitting on the kitchen counter.

"Excuse me, please," Huddy said.

"Excuse yourself. I'm sleepin. Now beat it," the rude can opener said.

"I'm finished, Bessy. That can opener was too grouchy to tell me anything. I guess I might not be real jolly if somebody woke me up this late either," Huddy said.

"What's this?" Bessy asked as she picked up an envelope that was sticking out from under the can opener. It was an airplane ticket to Brazil. Bessy put it back where she found it. "That's odd. Let's try Snolly's room again. We might find more clues there, if we can get to it," Bessy said.

"Look, Bessy," Huddy said. Bessy turned and looked on the wall. It was another calendar with a dog driving a car.

"They must be popular," Bessy said. "I guess Mr. Steamy likes more than hot dogs, huh?"

"I guess so," Huddy agreed. Then the two left the kitchen and headed to Wartella Snollygoster's room.

Chapter 22

Bessy and Huddy had no trouble getting into Wartella's room since the classroom doors didn't have locks. When Bessy went in, she noticed a bad smell in the air. "You can tell this is Snolly's room. It smells just like her," Bessy said. Bessy walked over to Wartella's desk and took her flashlight out. "Oh, no," she said.

"What's wrong?" Huddy asked.

"The batteries are dead."

"Why don't you just turn the ceiling lights on?"

"If I did that, Huddy, old cat face or the police might see us in here. I don't want to call the police until I find THE. And I don't want to call cat face at all."

"I have an idea."

"Let's hear it," Bessy said.

"Why don't you plug me in and use my light. It's bright, but not too bright."

"That's a good idea. Do you know where an outlet is?"

"There should be one by Snolly's desk if I remember right."

Bessy looked for the outlet. "You're right, Huddy. Here it is," Bessy said. She then plugged Huddy in and used his light to see.

"Here's another one of those calendars," Huddy said. It was on Wartella Snollygoster's desk.

"I never would've thought she'd be the type to have a calendar with a dog driving a car on it. She's too mean to be funny," Bessy said.

"Look at all the notes she's written on it," Huddy said.

Bessy read aloud. "Be mean to Uncle Joe. Real Hard Test. Super Hard Quiz. Yell at class all hour. Throw something at someone. Golly," Bessy said. "She's got the rest of her life planned out."

"It looks like it," Huddy said. "Don't you like these calendars, Bessy?"

"Yeah, they're O.K."

"Don't they look familiar?"

"I thought I'd seen this kind of a calendar somewhere before. I've got one of these on my desk. Grace's dad was nice enough to give everybody in the school one. Look at the top." Above the dog driving the car it was written out in black letters: Hey Rover, See Mr. Dover! Jack Dover, Locksmith. I've got the key to your problems.

"I think we can leave now, Huddy," Bessy said.

"Rarrrr! I don't think so," said the black panther as it walked into the room.

Chapter 23

The black panther came closer to Bessy. Bessy picked Huddy up and shined his light in the panther's eyes. The panther fell to the ground temporarily blinded. "Rarrrrr!" it said. Bessy quickly unplugged Huddy and raced out of the room. She looked behind her as she ran towards the library. The panther had recovered and was chasing after her. "Rarrrr!" it said.

"Where should we go?" Huddy said as he shook with fear.

"I was thinking about the library. At least I'd have the home court advantage there," Bessy said as the panther gained on her.

"We might get trapped in there, though."

"I suppose you're right. Let's try to get to the car if we can."

Bessy and Huddy passed the library and continued to head towards her car. To slow the panther down, Bessy threw everything she had in her pockets behind her in the air. First she threw the flashlight, and it hit the beast in the head. This just made it even angrier. After the flashlight, Bessy threw some pocket change, and then the leather bag that she had her marbles in earlier. She was so scared that she threw things until there was nothing left in her pockets at all except the note she had found in the office. Finally, Bessy and Huddy got to the car. Bessy tried to open the door. She forgot that she had locked it.

"Hurry up, Bessy!" Huddy said. "Fang Face is right behind us."

"I know. I'm hurrying," Bessy said as she reached down into her pants pocket to get her keys. "Oh, no!"

"Oh, no what?" Huddy asked.

"You know when I was throwing all that stuff in the hallway?"

"Yeah, what about it?"

"I think I accidentally threw my car keys at that panther."

"Oh, no." Just then the panther came outside and headed towards Bessy and Huddy. It smiled as it held out its paw. There in the palm of its hand were Bessy's keys.

"Rarrrr!" the panther said as it came closer and closer to Bessy and Huddy. Bessy didn't know what to do but run, so she began running around her red station wagon while the panther with her car keys chased her and Huddy.

"Hey, Big Red! Are you awake?" Huddy yelled as the panther chased Bessy and him around the car. "Who's Big Red?" Bessy asked Huddy with a gasp.

"Your car, Bessy."

"I'm up. I'm up," Big Red, the car said. "Need some help?"

"We sure do, Big Red," Huddy said.

"Sure thing, dude," the car said. As Bessy and Huddy passed one of the car doors it suddenly unlocked and opened. The door hit the panther right in the belly and knocked it down. "Quick! Get in!" the car said. Bessy hopped in the car with Huddy, shut the door, and locked it.

"So you talk too, car?" Bessy said.

"Yep, I sure do, sugar," the car said.

"I guess you can start without the keys. Can't you?" Bessy said.

"Yeah, I can, sugar," the car said.

"Go for it then, Big Red," Huddy said as the black panther got up and ran back over towards the car.

"I can't. Look at my gas gauge," the car said. Bessy and Huddy looked at the gas gauge. Its arrow was on empty.

"I'm sorry, guys. This whole thing is my fault," Bessy said. "I always mess things up. I guess I can't do anything right."

"Oh, Bessy," Huddy said as the panther began beating on the window outside. "Don't ever give up."

"What can I do?" Bessy said as she dropped her head on the steering wheel and began to cry. Bessy's head hit the steering wheel so hard that the horn sounded. The loud noise frightened the panther, and it jumped away from the car. When Bessy went to lift her head off the horn, it continued to blow. The horn was stuck.

"Now I got the horn stuck," Bessy said.

"That might be good, Bessy," Huddy said. "Maybe someone will come and help us."

"Why didn't I think of that?" Big Red said. As the horn sounded, the angry panther came back over to the car and began beating even harder on the window.

"Open this door," the panther said.

"Not by the hair of my chinny chin chin," Bessy said. Then, from out of nowhere a four legged snowball with black spots pounced on top of the giant panther and began fighting him. It was the dalmatian that had been in Bessy's car and chewed her good purse up.

"Good grief," Bessy said. "This is like <u>The Hound of the Baskervilles</u>."

"Let's get the police, Bessy," Huddy said.

"You stay here, Huddy. I'll run faster if I don't have to carry you," Bessy said. "Big Red. Keep an eye on Huddy. Lock him in when I leave."

"I'll take care of him," Big Red said as Bessy jumped out and shut the car door.

"Good luck, Bessy," Huddy said.

Chapter 24

Bessy ran with all her might while the dog, that she was now happy to see, wrestled with the panther. Before Bessy entered the school, she yelled to the dog, "Do to him what you did to my purse!" Then she went inside the building and ran to the office. By the time Bessy got to the office, she was panting. She went to open the door, but it wouldn't budge.

"That panther's locked the door," Bessy said. "Now what am I going to do?" Bessy slammed her hand against the wall in frustration.

Ding! Ding! Ding!

She had done it! Bessy had hit the fire alarm. Bessy turned and ran back outside again where she found the dalmatian still attacking the panther. She was glad that dogs hated cats. Within minutes the Balloonsboro Fire Department pulled up to the school. When they saw their pet in a fight with the giant panther, they called the dog off and began to drown the panther by squirting it with their fire hoses until it was lying flat on the ground completely unconscious. With Bessy's help, the firemen then tied the overgrown cat up with some rope they had so it wouldn't get away. The cat burglar had been nabbed.

Chapter 25

B essy was hugging the dalmatian as Mr. Jacobs and the police pulled up in front of the school. The dog that she had considered a pest was now her hero.

"What's going on here, Bessy?" Mr. Jacobs shouted after he got out of his car and walked over to Bessy. The police were right behind him.

"Just a minute, Joe," Bessy said. She ran over to her car to get Huddy. She came back carrying him by the handle. "Let me know if I forget to tell them something, Huddy."

"I sure will, Bessy," the projector said.

"Would you mind telling me what's going on?" Mr. Jacobs asked.

"Tell us, too," one of the policemen said as everybody gathered around Bessy and Huddy.

"It all started tonight at about midnight when I came down to the library and discovered that The Adventures of Huckleberry Finn was missing," Bessy said. "I didn't want to upset anybody, so I thought I'd try to locate it by myself. I guess I needed a little help after all. I evidently forgot to turn the alarm back on after I put the book back in the security case."

"You mean you took the book out? You were only to do that in an emergency, Bessy," Mr. Jacobs said.

"I know, but as an Official Librarian, I thought it was an emergency. That book needed to get out a while. Would you like to be locked up like a wild animal all of the time?"

"No," Mr. Jacobs said.

"Well, that book needed to get out for a while. An Official Librarian knows these things. So I took the book out, and I forgot to turn the alarm back on when I put it back. When I stopped by here tonight, the book was gone. You can imagine how upset and worried I was, so I searched the school until I believe I know who the culprit is."

"Who is it?" Mr. Jacobs asked as everyone listened.

"It's that panther," Bessy said. "I wondered who could have tried to steal the book all night. Jane Blab and Wartella Snollygoster were both good suspects. I even thought the vice-principal might have stolen it. That's why I happen to be wearing his gorilla suit. I put it on to compare this costume's prints with the prints that the panther made. They didn't match, though, and I got this zipper stuck. Anyway, if you remove the panther's head, which I think is a costume too, you should see Grace Dover, the secretary."

"Surely not Grace?" Mr. Jacobs said.

"Let's see," one of the policemen said as he walked over to the panther who was tied up. The officer unzipped the head of the panther and pulled it off. It was Grace Dover. She looked down at the ground.

"Grace. How could you?" Mr. Jacobs said.

She didn't say anything.

Bessy continued. "I never would've thought Grace would do such a thing, but I put a few clues together. First of all, I noticed there were no locks on the library window. Somebody had just taken them off recently. Who would know more about locks than a locksmith or his daughter? My aunt told me that Grace was as good at working with locks as her dad was. I forgot all about her locksmith ability until I noticed all the calendars in the school advertising her dad's locksmith services. She also had written a note asking the security company for another key. I found an unfinished copy of it wadded up on the office floor. Evidently, someone interrupted her and she tried to throw it in the trash can. I guess it fell out. The letter said to send the extra key to 109 Ma. I didn't know what 109 Ma was for a while. Then it came to me. She was going to have it sent to her house, 109 Maple Street. She just didn't get the address finished. The fact that she wasn't at home tonight when I went to her house made me suspect her. To keep me from messing her plan up, she tried to scare me away by wearing that panther suit."

"You're too smart for your own good, Bessy," Grace said with a frown.

"Where's the book?" Mr. Jacobs asked.

"Grace should know," Bessy said.

"I don't know where it is. When I came to get it the case was already empty," Grace whined.

"Don't lie," Mr. Jacobs said.

"I'm not," Grace said. "Why should I lie? You caught me. I couldn't sell the thing now even if I did have it."

"Why did you want to steal it in the first place?" a policeman asked.

"That's easy," Bessy said. "Grace wanted to buy new clothes. Her husband wouldn't let her buy anything new. He must be a real penny pincher. My aunt even said so. I bet she was planning on running away to South America after she sold the book for who knows how much. She got Mr. Steamy to pick up her plane ticket for Brazil by buying him a sack of cheeseburgers. That way nobody would see her at the travel agency and get suspicious. I found her ticket in the kitchen under the can opener. I guess Mr. Steamy didn't have time to give it to her yet."

"Is that true, Grace?" Mr. Jacobs asked.

"Yes, yes, it's true," Grace said.

"So where's the book?" the principal asked.

"I really don't know," Grace said. "It was gone before I got to it. I thought Bessy had it hidden somewhere."

"I sure don't know either," Bessy said as a blue car drove up.

"Where is it then? Is it lost?" Mr. Jacobs said as he put his hand on his forehead.

A small boy got out of the blue car. "Hey, Bessy!" he said. It was Idunno.

"Who's that?" a policeman asked Bessy.

"Idunno," she said.

"I don't believe I do either," the police officer said.

"I heard all the police and firemen were coming here on our scanner," Idunno said. "They mentioned your name, Bessy. Are you O.K.?"

"I'm just fine, Idunno, but I'm afraid I've lost The Adventures of Huckleberry Finn," Bessy said.

"No you didn't," Idunno said. "I thought I'd get a book to read before I went home yesterday, but you had left early and locked the library doors, so I just came in the window like I used to do last year when the other librarian was here. When I saw that the alarm was off, I thought I'd better take the book home so nobody would steal it. I didn't want you to get in trouble or anything, Bessy."

"How did you know the window would be unlocked, Idunno?" Mr. Jacobs asked.

"It used to always be open, but then the janitor put a lock on it right before school was out. I happened to notice that somebody had taken the lock off today when I was helping Bessy. I didn't mean to cause any trouble."

"You didn't," Bessy said as she hugged the little boy.

"So where's the book?" Mr. Jacobs asked again.

"It's at home on my coffee table," Idunno said.

"That's all right, Mr. Jacobs," Bessy said. "I can get it on the way home."

"O.K., Bessy," Mr. Jacobs said. "Just take care of it."

"I will, don't worry. After all, I am an Official Librarian."

After the police took Grace Dover away, everybody else left too. Bessy and Huddy got in the car with Idunno and his dad and headed to his house where they went inside and found THE watching T.V.

"Come on in, Bessy," the book said. "There's a real neat movie coming on called The Return of the Cat Burglar.

Bessy just laughed.

Dear Reader,

Below is a scavenger hunt I made that only the best readers can complete. I bet you can't.

Yours truly,

The Panther

^^^

Beware!!!
The Panther's Scavenger Hunt

* See if you can find the following things:

1. The first mentioning of the protagonist's full name

2. An example of alliteration

3. An allusion

4. A reference to trains

5. An example of foreshadowing

Describe it!

* Find and record descriptions of the following:

1. Bessy's appearance when she arrives at school the first day

2. The library when Bessy first arrives

3. The school office

Tell me!

* Using the text, answer the questions. Support what you say with persuasive explanations.

1. Which character in the story is your favorite?

2. Would you like to be a student at Ballonsboro High School?

Breinigsville, PA USA
21 October 2009
226205BV00001B/1/P